The Cyclist's Tale

and other short cycling stories

For Anka

First Edition − 2016

Copyright © 2016 Kevin R. Haylett

Editor: Graham Theakston

Cover photograph by Bernard Thompson
printed with permission.

Typeset in Bembo

The Cyclist's Tale

and other short cycling stories

Kevin R. Haylett

Preface

Cycling can be brutal, with cold winds, rain, inconceivable distances, fatigue and pain. But that's just a minor part. The joy, sublime pleasure and experience of life are given back to the rider by a simple bicycle, the journey, the road ahead.

Glossy magazines and television adverts sell drivers a fantasy of freedom, only to deliver ever–growing queues of traffic, while cycling gives life. If you are a cyclist, you know this.

Riding is intoxicating, it rewards with wonderful days, journeys and friends. It's a pastime, a job of work, a sport, a love, and a passion that gives and gives again.

The advert becomes real, as you cycle through perfect sunny lanes and along coastlines that go on forever, or over the highest mountains with the sweetest descents.

This collection of stories is a fiction. Clubs, characters and names are assigned. There may be truths. Somebody you recognise, a friend, yourself, the road. But that is your imagination.

When riding, ideas and inventions come alive. Minutes, hours and days become miles, as games played in the mind give way to peace. These stories come from the roads, the hills and mountains. From cold winter training to dancing on pedals on a Mediterranean island. From riding the high peaks of the Alps and Pyreneans to the Blue Ridge Mountains of North Carolina. Dip in after a cold winter ride, as you would a hot bath or shower, or even after long miles in the warmth of the sun. Maybe, somewhere, you are here, in these pages?

Contents

Friends

Mike's head hurt. Dubrowski had brought them both down. It had happened fast. Without Dubrowski, Mike couldn't have kept up with the pack. Working together they had both held on. Before the crash they had pushed up the main field, crested the climb and were on the descent. Dubrowski had dropped back and caught his wheel. Maybe. Who really knows what happens in a race? They'd both come down, with a few others. No, it wasn't Dubrowski's fault. Mike remembered the mutt.

1

Dubrowski, the old pro, took everything in his stride, and put up with Mike's outbursts. They'd found a good way of working together and could push each other along at just the right moments. They both lay there on the black top.

"Go on. Get up, deck him." Bill chided Mike on and pointed to Dubrowski, who was already lying next to him on the tarmac. "He knocked you off!"

The last time Mike had followed Bill's advice, he'd had to leave his club: If 'leave' describes being kicked out. It had taken months to find a new club and settle in and he didn't want to screw it up again. The problem wasn't just Bill, there was also Dave. Together the pair baited him, he was their puppet. The mutt would run alongside, snarling and snapping at his ankles.

"Hit him, hit him." Dave was shouting and Bill had also joined in.

"C'mon, get up, hit him."

Bill's eyes were bloodshot, his face angular; teeth gleamed under a razor like grin. Dave and Bill's words were harsh and bitter, they cut deep, and all with a sickening look. The mutt, rabid, drooled from the mouth. The two always wore the same jerseys, and rode the same bikes.

Mike couldn't remember them not being around. They always rode with him. Bill, smiling, with the flashing teeth and Dave with his sickening laugh. Bill had the trick of it. Whenever Mike started to feel confident and ride well, Bill would knock him down with a comment. Sharp, straight to the point.

"You've not got it! Why the hell did you think you could be a cyclist?" Bill spat the words out through his teeth.

Dave wasn't any more subtle.

"You're going to give up again, aren't you? You should, you're shit." Dave laughed at him and smiled with his sickly smile.

Mike wasn't going to hit Dubrowski. Bill and Dave could shout all they like. He stared up at Bill and Dave from the ground. They looked down at him, spitting venom. Today he could ignore them. It wasn't always the case. Sometimes there were more of Bill, Dave and the mutt, than himself.

It was worse preparing for a race. Everything had to be just right; clothing, tyre pressures, food, and the weather. From the moment he started looking over the bike, to laying his head on the pillow, Bill and Dave gave a running commentary on his actions. It was relentless: 'Why did he think he could race?', 'How many times had he been beaten that year?', 'Didn't he feel like shit?', 'What was the point?'. While adjusting the gears, Bill and Dave would lean over, closer. Dave laughed and Bill spat his words out, flashing his teeth. The mutt strained and snarled on a leash.

Of course they weren't there. Mike knew it. They were just figments of his imagination, twisted neurones in his brain deciding to fire.

Alcohol sometimes helped, but it changed him, and then he didn't like himself. Bill, Dave, and the mutt faded into a dream, but so did life. Eventually he'd stop drinking. Mike needed to wake up, to come up for air. Even if it did mean facing *them*. Life felt like a tightrope, maybe he should jump off.

Both Dubrowski and Mike had been preparing hard for the season's big race. It wasn't the longest, but it was going to be tough. One of those where the organisers find every steep climb, string them into a single ride and laugh as the riders punish themselves. They could do that, and do it well. Last year, Dubrowski came in second on the same course, and he was close behind. It was one of his best results of the season and maybe they could do better.

The last few weeks had been about training, training and more training. Honing their condition. Work had disappeared into race preparation and planning. During the days, he'd keep his chest strap on and watch his heart rate. Slowly, the rate was dropping, his fitness improving. Bill and Dave's incessant diatribe became worse and worse.

"It'll make no difference." Bill's eyes were even more bloodshot than usual. Dave sniggered.

"No chance."

Peering up at them both, Mike wondered where the mutt was, it had been unusually quiet. Thoughts repeat. Maybe if he focused hard enough they would go away. It didn't work. He'd tried everything. Yoga, meditation, drugs and getting drunk.

The only thing that really worked, was pushing hard on the bike. Then, when he had the focus, when all that mattered was the effort and pain in his legs, at that moment they were gone. As long as he could crank the pedals, his mind would clear. With each moment, delivered with an agony of effort, he would be alone. It didn't last, it couldn't.

They would quickly be back, as they leaked through into his world and were soon as real as anything else. Of course, nobody else could see them. They were just a part of him, faulty wiring. An imbalance of chemicals.

Bill and Dave had both arrived, from thin air, right after the crash and now stood over Mike. The mutt was growling. Mike lay on the side of the road and watched Dubrowski get up from the black top and come over to check him out. Dubrowski's mouth was moving, there was no sound. Looking down, towards his feet, Mike could see the rips on his jersey and blood from the grazes on his legs. Road rash. Nothing too bad. Mike's helmet lay on the road. Crushed on one side.

"Keep that mutt off me, did you see him jump out at me?" Mike shouted out. Dubrowski looked puzzled. Of course! The bloody dog wasn't real.

What had happened? He could just remember

topping the climb. His heart rate had been on the limit. That's right, he'd managed to take the lead on the last section. A foggy memory, Dubrowski was still looking down at him, mouthing more words. Mike had started the descent and was making good progress. Descending wasn't Mike's strongest skill but he'd stayed ahead. Just. About a third of a mile down, recovering from the climb, the mutt had jumped out at him from the hedgerow. He flinched. The bike slipped an inch, Dubrowski's wheel touched his and they were both down. And a few others behind.

Mike could just make out Dubrowski's words.

"There's an ambulance on the way, don't move. You've taken a knock on the head."

The race was over. He could see Dave out of the corner of his eye, in hysterics, laughing at him. Bill was grinning with his teeth shining. The mutt snarled.

His wrist was sore, maybe fractured. No major breaks. They stopped him getting up.

"Best wait." Dubrowski smiled, warmly.

It wasn't Mike's first trip in an ambulance. The two hour wait in emergency was another endurance event. Each second stretching into eternity with the clock finally advancing another minute. Somebody gave him a morphine injection for the pain in his wrist. With the world numbed, Bill, Dave and the mutt became quiet.

After being cleaned up and given a couple of stitches, the doctor wanted to do a scan on his head. There was a big bruise on his right temple. It was hospital policy, they had to do a scan. Mike had been concussed and out for a good five minutes on the roadside.

It would be another hour before the scanner was available. Did he want a drink? The freedom he'd felt on the road just a few hours earlier could barely be remembered. Mike could see himself cresting the climb having shaken off the chasing group, and then again remembered Bill, Dave and the mutt.

The scanner, a giant metal doughnut, used an equally giant magnet. A nurse had given him earplugs. Now he lay there with his head in a box, in the doughnut. The drum—beat of the magnet switching back and forth seeped through the plugs in his ears. It magnetised the water in his head. It was simple. The magnet would switch on. Parts of the water molecules would line up and when the magnet switched off they could pick up the tiny little magnetic signals made as they returned to normal. The signals could be turned into a picture.

Kerbang, bang, bang! The giant magnet switched on and off, over and over again. Even with the earplugs it was still loud. After a long time, it stopped.

Later, two doctors showed him the pictures of his brain. There was nothing wrong. Everything was fine. Just another confirmation that he was okay. Afterwards, Mike was finally allowed home.

Dr Lee always checked the scans. The image caught her eye. There was something unusual in the blood vessels. She had passed over the image once and found herself returning to it. Unconsciously she'd noticed something.

It wasn't to do with the injury. It was something pathological; bodies were never the same. They were as different on the inside as the outside. Organs could be displaced, positions changed.

It wasn't so unusual, but there it was. One of the arteries had a restriction. It was barely noticeable. She wasn't surprised it had been missed, the younger doctors wouldn't have been looking at that part of the brain.

Sometimes these restrictions were the result of a tumour. But not in this case, there were none of the tell-tale signs. The artery just looked narrower. It was unusual and probably had always been like that.

The patient was twenty-six with nothing in his

notes; although she didn't have the full set. There were no problems. The figures were good, as good as they could be. So it was just a different anatomy. Maybe it would make an article in the neuroradiology journal? She'd need permission from the patient.

The letter made Mike feel uneasy, they'd called him back. It didn't say why, there was just an appointment time. It frightened Mike, he'd been back on the bike for over two weeks. Surely there wasn't anything wrong. The appointment wasn't for a few weeks. No. It couldn't be anything serious.

"Any headaches? How's your eyesight? Have you ever fainted?" The questions took a while. They were delivered with cold routine.

Dave and Bill had been watching. The mutt barked. It was sharp and loud. Reflexively he told it to shut up, under his breath.

"Pardon?" The doctor looked surprised.

"I'm sorry, I'm a bit stressed and tend to talk to

myself, just ignore me." It was usually enough, but not this time. This time was different. There was a glimmer in the doctor's eyes as she moved her chair closer and shone a light into his eyes. The pupils contracted. Very carefully and softly she spoke again.

"Have you ever heard voices?"

"Pardon?" Mike flinched.

"Voices that others can't hear."

"What do you think? I've had a bump on my head and gone mad?" It was a stupid response. Mike felt embarrassed.

Dr Lee knew this was going to be difficult. Even if they had heard voices or had hallucinations, patients wouldn't admit it. It was like stepping on eggshells, overcoming centuries of fear. The fear of the madhouse, insanity. A fear so deep it was a fundamental part of the culture. Images and stories, language, all—pervasive and all creating a brick wall around the people who experience hallucinations.

Still, the talk came naturally. Gently, in a practised matter-of-fact way, she explained. The statistics were staggering.

"In the latest study, thirty eight percent had reported hallucinations. Almost three in every hundred had hallucinations more than once a week."

Dr Lee went on to explain that, surprisingly, hallucinations were pretty normal. Although most people said nothing. They occurred before falling asleep, *Hypnagogic hallucinations*. Few were afraid of the manifestations. They came and went.

Dr Lee talked in a soft tone, she could see that Mike was listening, following every word. Yes, she was certain, he was hallucinating. Probably right now. What was it he said under his breath? On finishing she asked if he had any questions. The patients rarely did, they were silent, lost in their own worlds or struggling to comprehend the alien world of the hospital.

"Why am I here? Have you found something

wrong with me?" Mike still wasn't really sure what the Doctor had said.

Dr Lee smiled gently, and explained about the constricted blood vessel. That, even with no symptoms, she would like to publish the results, and could she have his permission? His name wouldn't be mentioned.

So that was it. Mike leaned back in his chair. His palms were hot and sweaty against the armrests. He hadn't liked the questions about hearing voices or seeing things. The silence when she asked had been stifling. Mike had answered no, without a second thought. Dave was chuckling at him and Bill was walking around the room waving his hands in the air, emulating the doctor sitting in front of him. The mutt was scratching at the door.

So if there was nothing wrong, he could leave. Mike couldn't speak. His throat was dry, the mutt was glowering at him. No, he didn't hear and see things.

Yes, she could use the picture of his brain. As he left, he absently took the card that was being handed to him. The card had the doctors telephone number printed on it. Just in case.

So there was a choice. It had explained so much. The narrowing of the artery was causing *hypoxia*, lack of oxygen, to a small part of his brain. When Mike was cycling and pushing really hard it teased enough oxygen to stop the hallucinations. Bill, Dave and the mutt simply stopped existing.

It could be fixed. Dr Lee had said it was possible to push a small device into the vessel. It would be passed along a vein and eventually slipped into place. The device, a *stent*, would open up and force the walls open. The blood would flow more easily.

On the way home, Bill chided him, and Dave was laughing. The Mutt was growling and slobbering. He found himself talking to them. Life was pretty much back to normal.

On the next ride out, Mike pushed harder and harder. He was out on his own. Well, not really, Bill and Dave rode effortlessly beside him, shouting and cursing. They were riding just off his shoulder, on the same old bikes, wearing the same jerseys. They both shouted and cursed about how shit he was. For a brief moment he looked them in the eye.

The shouting and cursing didn't bother him, he was used to it. In a way they kept him going. They'd become his friends, almost always there, reliable, company. Mike pushed harder, his friends faded, becoming distant memories. Mike felt free, a weight had been lifted, but maybe he would miss them? The operation wasn't scheduled for another two weeks and he still had time to change his mind.

Climbing

Garvey frowned, there they were. He'd ventured the five metres in the crisp air to the garage, opened the door and stared. The two instruments of torture stood immobile, disdainful. There was ice on the roads, it was sleeting.

There was a time he'd have kitted up with longs, gloves, skull cap and a winter jacket and then gone out on his training bike. But two years earlier he'd pulled himself out of a ditch, stood up, and then fallen down again. Black ice! Garvey had decided there and then: Never again. With slips and slides he was forced to walk with his bike to a clear stretch of road. Humiliation.

Indoor trainers, the Turbo or the rollers? The rollers were old school, good for balance, and for getting your cadence up. Great for warming up. But really there was no choice, it was the Turbo. That's where you could put in a real effort. Windows at the far end of the garage reflected the fluorescent light against the winter's darkness.

It was all set up. As if heading out, he slipped a couple of bottles in their cages. Fuel for the efforts. Then Garvey switched on the TV, computer and cooling fans and selected the Alp. After ten minutes of warming up he pressed the green *'Go'* button. It was the routine, barely bearable. It wasn't really riding.

The television kept him company as he cycled up the Alp. An antiques program distracted him. Buying and selling. The cheery presenter was explaining how the contestants had just purchased a fake. They were going to need their bonus buy.

Warmed up, he was pushing some good power now. His best time for the Alp was forty eight minutes. Not far off the record; of course that was on a real road. The two giant fans, set each side, kept him cool. Sweat dripped onto the towel. Three or four times a week the garage became the road.

Garvey's thoughts wandered vaguely. Sometimes he could almost feel the wind, he was on the Alp ascending into crisp blue skies. Cornering a switchback, a thousand metres up. The road easing a little and then going up again. The valleys below. An auctioneer was now explaining that the fake pot may make some money. Garvey watched the figures on the computer screen. Wattage and time kept him company along with the profile of the mountain. He kept going. Now there was an image on the computer screen; a rider passed him. With a bit more effort, Garvey was matching the wheel in front.

On the television, the blue team had just made a loss, they were going to need their bonus buy. A woman was holding up a one—eyed Teddy Bear, a button in its ear. *Steiff.* The cheery presenter was suggesting it may be a good idea to choose the bonus buy.

Garvey pushed the pedals a little harder. The News would be on soon. His towel and bib shorts were soaked in sweat. Cycling? Even more sweat ran down his legs. And then, still in the garage, he was at the top of the Alp. The Alp d'Huez. The legend of the Tour. All 21 switchbacks had been conquered. He got off his bike, saved the results and switched off the computer.

The red team had lost money on the fake pot. Turning off the television, Garvey took the empty bottles from the cages, picked up the towel, switched off the light, and closed the garage door.

The club met at the Waltzing Weasel for a drink. Dubrowski was there with Mac and the newcomer. They were talking about hill climbing. Put a few cyclists together and at some point the subject will be hills. The new guy was thinking of doing the *Memorial Club Hill Climb*. It seemed a good idea. They always had one new challenger. Last year it had been Mac.

When climbing, you can't fool nature, the lighter riders can always take advantage. Power−to−weight was the key. All cyclists try to unlock the secret of the perfect climb. There were theories, techniques, books, videos. Coaches all espoused the best way to climb.

Mostly it was genetics, but ultimately it involved sweating and pushing the pedals around as hard and fast as you could. Around. Once you were pedalling squares you'd had it, the bike would be swinging from side to side with the rider out of the saddle. At the

Waltzing Weasel, with beer drunk, subjects spun from hills to cafés, to track nights and Mallorca in the spring: They had booked up with Doug, in S'Arenal, south of Palma. They would be part of the mass migration of cyclists heading south.

Winter, like the last two, had been harsh. It had been hard to get any time on the road. This left the daily visit to the Col Du Garage with the company of the red and blue team as they tried to find gold amongst the antiques shop and fairs. Garvey became an expert. While riding up the Galibier, he would be shouting at the telly 'not fifty pounds for *Weames ware* – you'll be lucky to make twenty.' The auctioneer later confirmed Garvey's estimate.

The bespectacled presenter suggested the team may need their bonus buy. This time some great hunk of Victorian luggage. Garvey exclaimed: 'not the luggage, it's junk!' Still pedalling up the Galibier, sweat dripped onto the floor of the garage.

Garvey looked from the computer with its figures of power, time and metres climbed, to the television. Lifting his gaze upwards he could see his reflection in the dark glass. The cold sharp winter hanging outside. It seemed a strange sight. So far from the open roads of Mallorca. As he pedalled, his thoughts wandered. Leaving the hotel at S'Arenal he turned left at the promenade just by Balneario Three, a local café.

Then to the roundabout and turning right on the 6014 to start the climb up the 'five mile' hill along the coast road. Then steady for a while, first passing the turn off for Cala Pi on the right. The next landmark was the café at the Talaiots Bronze Age megaliths, just at the twenty-three kilometre marker. Here he could turn left for Llucmayor or carry on. The next café was just another kilometre further on. It was always full of cyclists. Maybe a coffee there on the way back? One last caffeine hit for the race down to S'Arenal.

Today he'd keep going, up the coast road. Beyond the café, the open road stretched around the headlands, slowly heading up Santanyi. First past Sa Rapita, then Ses Salines and Ses Lombards and on. At Ses Salines he would stop at the garage, on the roundabout with the strange giant spring sculpture in the middle. Now looking into the distance, you could see the Monastery San Salvador on its own mountain.

Few cars travelled on this road, they had just laid new tarmac. There was a bunch up ahead. He was reeling them in. Then he'd sit at the back for a while and recover. After a short while, with good legs, he'd then go off the front. Steadily he'd make his way to Porto Colom and then onto Porto Christo. It was a steady ride, one he knew well.

Awakened by the beep of the computer, the tension eased in his legs, he had finished the ascent of the Col Du Galibier. The 'road' had flattened out. The computer displayed Garvey's time, heart rate, and the energy he had used. The credits were rolling across the antiques show on the television.

Winters can be slow for cyclists. But the new season arrives quickly and the February Mallorca training camp marks its start. Garvey was always anxious about taking his bike with him. The civilians collect their luggage, a carousel number is announced on the display. Bikes are collected at number sixteen. Not a carousel, a conveyor for bikes and oversized luggage. Garvey would wait nervously for the airport to give birth. Finally, with a great relief, Garvey's baby was delivered safely.

From arrival, cyclists soon settle into the routines of daily cycling. A large breakfast to fuel up for the day. Then meeting up in the morning outside the hotel. The route? Maybe it was decided the night before in Los Olivos or the Timbol café? Maybe a medal ride?

Days are quickly filled by open roads, hundreds of kilometres, cafés, and nights in the bar. Sometimes, a big ride out over the mountains. This was the stuff of cycling. Escape, a retreat. Efforts are laid bare on the roads. Camaraderie and fellowship. Kids riding their bikes. Training.

After a few days of riding, Dubrowski, Mac and Garvey had settled on the Sa Calobra climb. It was a medal ride, so came with something to take home.

The Sa Calobra, officially Coll de Cal Reis, is a ten kilometre drop into a tiny fishing port. The climb of six hundred and sixty–eight metres has twenty–six hairpin turns with an average gradient of seven percent.

The climb has a couple of problems. First, you have to get to it. That involves cycling up the Coll de Sa Batalla from Selva and then turning right on the MA10 and climbing to the top of Sa Calobra. Then you descend down to the port, to come back up the same way. The only other way back was by sea ferry.

All three looked down the mountain, they had

stopped to try and spot the port. The descent was tricky. The hairpins were tight and both cyclists and cars were trying to get down to the port. At points there was only one lane. Rocky outcrops overhung the road. Every now and then a coach would push and squeeze through, stopping and blocking the road. They took the descent easy, with hands on brakes and riding together. The switchbacks kept coming, a realisation started to hit. There was absolutely no choice. They all had to cycle back up. Normally a climb came with a descent, a sweet reward for the work done. But this descent was far from sweet, creating anxiety, even for the best descenders. Eventually they arrived at the port.

Garvey felt anxious, uncomfortable, he just wanted to get the climb over with. Mac, by far the best climber and lightest of them all, was excited. Dubrowski seemed calm enough. A quick pee. Garvey squeezed out an energy gel. Nerves. Surely it was just another climb. Seven percent, not so steep. Mac and Dubrowski gave each other the look, and nodded towards Garvey. Garvey was the club champion, he'd be first up. The climb waited. Garvey was first to speak:

"Okay, okay let's get it done."

In Mallorca, February was cool, the air clear. The rocks above cut into the blue Mediterranean sky. The scenery was stunning, everything a cyclist dreams of. A challenge, friends to ride with, a moment to really feel alive. This was what cycling in Mallorca was about. Except Garvey felt miserable, his legs felt like shit, his heart rate was far too high and to make things worse, both Mac and Dubrowski were already one switchback ahead of him.

"Shit." He was struggling to breathe, he muttered under his breath. "For Christ's sake Garvey, ease into it."

It seemed to take forever, slowly his mind wandered. He looked down at his watch, twelve forty—five. What would he be doing back home? Sure, it was February, there was still snow on the roads. He'd be in the garage on the Turbo, Garvey could see the computer screen in front of him with the watts, distance, and profile of the climb.

Garvey's heart rate started to lower, his body more comfortable. He could picture the *Weames ware* being sold at the auction. The blue team had lost thirty pounds and were going to take the bonus buy, it was that crappy Victorian luggage. He smiled to himself. He looked up at the road, there was Dubrowski.

"Hey Dub." Dubrowski was looking into the mid distance, hardly noticing Garvey pass. Garvey thought he saw a nod.

And still Garvey found himself back in the garage, the bow—tied presenter highlighting the values of a picture, painted for Victorians on their Grand European Tour. Apparently the painters would make up a landscape with rocks and stones and bits of broccoli to represent the trees, a goat was painted, a shaft of light pierced the clouds. It was formulaic.

Garvey was passing Mac now! And smiling. He could see the irony, here he was on a classic of cycling climbs and all he could think about was antiques. He could even picture the rollers and turbo in the garage. Garvey's breathing was easy. His legs, light and strong, pushed him upwards.

Passing quite a few riders, his pace was surprisingly high. The tightness in his chest had melted away. Garvey stepped up out of the saddle, giggling a little at the thought of the Col Du Garage.

The next rider gave him a high five as he passed. Garvey was relaxed, he started appreciating the Sa Calobra for what it was, a beautiful captivating ride. Moments to be lost and never regained. As he rounded the last hairpin, the one with little car park, he noticed the tension of the climb in his legs ease. Garvey looked down at the hairpins to see if he could see Mac or Dubrowski. They were going to be a while.

That wasn't the last climb of the day. The three still had to climb the Puig and Soller before heading back to S'Arenal. Mac and Dubrowski were sure Garvey had given them a head start. Garvey was quiet.

That night they celebrated the ride with a few beers in the Timbol café. They had their medals. All slept well with tired legs. In the morning, a big breakfast. They were going to need it, it was going to be a hard ride.

Sports scientists research the effect of focus and distraction on cycling performance. So far results are largely inconclusive. However, some individuals do appear to benefit from distraction.

Headphones

In cycling there are rules to be broken. Old and new schools sit side by side. A helmet protects the brain and mind, a necessity for many. For others, a small cap serves as a reminder of freedom and simpler times. The calls of the bunch, a bark, 'car up', 'car back', arms wave like the shouts of a mime. Lids, potholes and gravel are announced with a gesture passed down the line.

Headphones are neatly tucked into jersey pockets with gels and keys. For many, headphones are an affront. And they were always a firm fixture of the club café debate. How can they be safe? A car drives by, delivering a passing symphony of rock, or was it Vivaldi?

Surely, cycling is to hear the sound of the roads? But some listen to music, the news, a chat show, a play, a stirring anthem or even a book. And sometimes nothing as they wait for a call or just protect their ears from the wind.

How had he got into racing? How long ago was it? The routines of training, club rides, preparation and racing had long since blurred these memories. As if descending the Galibier or infamous Tourmalet with fixed focus, the curves are mastered, the brakes seldom touched. The road disappears behind and is soon forgotten. Necessity keeps the mind ahead.

Of course he didn't often win, he wasn't a sprinter, and at seventy five kilos far too heavy to climb. But he could be there at the end. There was always the chance, the lure, the carrot, the hope. With the right touch and turn he could win.

In pro races an earpiece connects the riders to the manager, the *directeur sportif;* they are accepted. Safety calls are announced and strategies are agreed over the hidden waves. Temporary alliances are made only to be broken at a whim, nature calls are agreed. An amnesty, a temporary peace, is declared as needs must.

A small piece of tape holds the earphone in one ear. Sometimes a rider pulls the earphone out in disgust at the instructions. Come back to the bunch, ease off, drop back. Help a failing rider. All are fair and part of the game. But not if your legs are good and today could be the day. For the amateurs there was no earpiece.

A cycle race is far beyond a game of chess. Bodies trained to the limit, a necessity, are not enough. Strategy, courage, a team, and nerve are all required. For hours and hours leads are defended, muscles exhausted. Then, in less than an instant, the race is lost or won as opportunity begs a chance to be taken. Opponents battle rivals, giving up the chance of a win as an outsider slips past. Races can be lost on an ego.

Today's race was following the season's pattern. He could see Garvey beginning to drop to the back of the bunch. There was no ego when Garvey decided he was on for the win. It had reduced the season down to the bunch scrapping for second places.

Garvey would sit in pack for most of the race, and with about thirty kilometres to go, would drop to the back.

Then heading back up to the front, Garvey would announce he was going off the front in a few kilometres

"If you want to join me?"

A few riders would look up and think about it; for less than a moment. Eyes would settle back on the wheel in front. Was it to psych them out? Maybe, but they knew. They couldn't hold Garvey's back wheel. He would soon be gone. Up the road. Goodbye, *hasta la vista*. Maybe there was a chance for second place?

Just as Garvey had said, at the base of the last climb, or on a bend or wherever he had decided that day. Garvey would rise out of the saddle a fraction, sit down and with what seemed utter ease, his pace would increase. Within a few seconds he was ahead. In a few more he became distant. Those at the front could see him putting his earphones in. It was as if he was going out on an afternoon jolly. They could complain about the headphones. But why? Even for those that could look up, the race was over.

He hadn't come second or third. Fourth. It wasn't bad. He'd ridden well, working with a small group that had managed a breakaway in the last ten kilometres. He'd feinted lack of energy, sucking wheel for the last two kilometres. Saving his legs. But it wasn't enough. He wasn't a sprinter, the legs just wouldn't go any faster. There was no kick, no final surge. Nothing. Still, fourth. Something to talk about in the pub.

Turning into the Waltzing Weasel's car park, Garvey was already putting his bike on a car rack. Garvey looked across, patting his legs.

"Good legs today."

A few of the other riders slid by. One or two patting Garvey on the back with a 'well done'. Garvey looked tired, his eyes a little bloodshot. There was always a cost. Even for Garvey.

The earpieces hung around Garvey's neck. The question begged itself. Pointing to invisible headphones around his own neck

"Anything good?" The words hung in the air.

Garvey gave a simple nod and an almost vacant response.

"Nah, nothing really, nothing." Just enough to acknowledge and close the question at the same time.

Some, with bikes now racked or dismantled and booted, were now heading into the pub for a drink. Garvey was already heading home. One drink: that would help. The session wasn't long, a few recapturing the last moments, the sprint for second place. The pack had rounded the corner almost capturing the breakaway. Reminders of the race were starting to be felt as legs begin to ache. Food is eaten, beer is drunk. Pretty much that's how it goes. And that was that.

Another race. The sweat was dripping from Jamie's jersey. He had given everything in the last climb. Just before, Garvey had drifted to the back, told everyone he was going at the next hill, and then dropped everyone. Again! But this time Jamie was going to keep Garvey in his sights.

If only he could hold the pace. It wouldn't be long, Jamie was on his limit, he'd break soon and Garvey would be away. The bunch would roll past, his legs would wither. But, what the hell, he wasn't going to win the sprint and nobody else was mad enough to try. And today his legs had felt good. Really good.

Up ahead Garvey was rummaging in his jersey pocket. There it was. Dragging out the earphones, he popped them in his ears. It looked effortless. It wasn't, and his bike weaved. Then with a slight adjustment Garvey was gone, and that really was that.

The bunch rolled past Jamie, a few nodded. A touch of the shoulder. They all knew. He'd had to try, it could have been Jamie's day. It wasn't but it could've been. Any of them would have tried, with good legs. Now digging deep, it was all Jamie could do to hang on at the back of the bunch, sucking wheel.

Dubrowski, an old pro, had dropped back to keep Jamie company:

"*Chapeau*, I thought you had him there."

Their eyes met. It was a compliment, but they both knew the truth.

"We need a beer." Dubrowski held up an

imaginary pint, they did. But there were still twelve kilometres to go with five on a climb. At the end of a race, time on a bike hangs like a lead balloon.

They were well back and late rolling into the car park. Garvey's bike was stashed and Garvey was doing stretches by his car. He raised a hand as they unclipped from their bikes and put them against the wall. It was as if Garvey had been waiting for them to come in:

"That was a great effort Jamie! You almost had my wheel back there. Just a bit more and you could have sat on and had a breather."

"Maybe." Jamie's response was tired and quiet. The effort had been painful.

Leaving the door open to his car, Garvey announced he was off inside for a pee. Dubrowski saw it first; Garvey's music player and headphones were on the seat.

"Go on Jamie!" Encouragingly, Dubrowski motioned to the music player:

"Take a listen? I'll keep a look out."

There had been a lot of speculation about the player's contents in the club, it was a hot topic on the café stop agenda. It was a rare opportunity, he'd have to be quick.

Pushing the earpieces firmly in, the palms of his hands itched. There was no sound, just noise. Jamie was sure he'd pressed play. There, something. Layers of sound in the noise.

A shout. It cut through the noise.

"Are you all right?"

There was deep pain in his chest. His arm. He could see the bone protruding. Adrenalin was wearing off, the agony was taking over. He wanted to stop the sobbing but he couldn't. He remembered hearing the crunch of the bone breaking just before the slap of his helmet crashing on the tarmac. Looking up, the voice again, loudly:

"You've had an accident!"

Blue flashing lights in his periphery. A nurse? Maybe a Doctor? They touched his arm. Detached, he could hear his own scream, what else could he do, electricity shot up his arm.

"We're going to give you something for the pain."

The pain. Jamie was going to be sick. Yesterday, today, when was this? The sounds drifted. He glimpsed down at the scar on his wrist; a year of rehabilitation.

Another deeper sound, he was lying in his bed burying his head in the pillow. Screams from the room below, his mother. Agony. Beyond the pain of birth, she was dying, the cancer aggressive. Her sobs echoed in his ears. The pillow wasn't enough. How did his Dad cope sleeping in the same room? He could hear him now.

"I'm here love, it will pass."

It didn't pass, even lying in bed gave her pain. Morphine helped, but not enough. The screams and sobs would cluster with a rhythm and then ebb away. It was too real and painful, he could feel himself collapsing. His mother was long dead? Five years. Was that true?

Sound. Another layer, deeper again.

Shock, he didn't want to be here. The last shell exploded thirty metres away and was still ringing in his ears. Jamie could taste acid and vomit in his mouth. Tommy was lying just left of the wall. The trench had protected them, but Tommy's leg was gone. The blood had drained from Tommy's face and his lips were pale blue.

"It's okay," Jamie spoke calmingly to Tommy and used a belt to tourniquet the bleeding leg.

Another explosion, the sound of silk as the air was cut by the shell, and then, crack, thunder, rain.

Not rain. Shrapnel and earth falling. Eyes sore, stinging with cordite and sulphur, struggled to make sense of a shaking world. Could anything make this stop? Then shouts, his own.

"Medic, Medic, over here!"

This was here and now, maybe hell, Jamie didn't want this. Now the edge of consciousness. When was this, where am I? Night terrors, a memory?

Now Jamie could hear the rolling of wheels on the tarmac. Where? When? Don't touch the brakes, not at this speed, ease off the power. The corner comes in sharp, too sharp. A bike is strewn on the road, a rider on the deck. Bunny hopping, and then slide. Now the burning pain of gravel burying itself into the skin and muscle. Jamie could hear his helmet sliding, scraping, breaking apart. They would be picking the gravel out of his leg later. He winced.

Adrenalin, slowly moving then checking. Nothing broken. Relief. Now to move the bike to the side of the road. The message had been sent, riders were slowing down before the corner. A motorcycle outrider was stepping off his bike with a first aid kit.

He could hear the heavy boots on the gravel, going to help.

The rider hadn't moved. Fear, and terror engulfed. Who was it? The rider was dead, the surrounding huddle silent. First aid was useless. Bending, the nausea, the bile, he wretched and heaved. The loss, screaming in his ears. An eternity of pain and suffering. It couldn't go on? Now shouts in a race radio, his hand went to the earphone in his ear, he pulled it out.

And back.

The pain eased. The Waltzing Weasel's car park was emptying, most were now in the pub with a beer. Dubrowski was staring and asked.

"Are you going to listen to it then?"

How long had passed? In some timeless moment, terror, fear and loss were there with him, no longer lost memories. But now they were quickly fading. With heart still pounding, Jamie's gut still twisted and his face was ashen. Jamie took the music player and headphones and walked the few paces back to Garvey's car where the door was still open. He put them back on the seat.

Catching site of Garvey heading back from the pub, he stepped away from the car and the headphones. Garvey looked at the open door to where the player lay and looked up. Bloodshot eyes met.

"Maybe next time." Garvey sounded sincere.

With battle lines still drawn across their faces they both relaxed and gave the nod. The nod of recognition. The acknowledgement of the cost; the pain, effort and demons that drove them both. Demons that sat on their shoulders screaming in their ears to lose themselves, to fight, to give all, to win, to escape and to ride.

Dubrowski, the old pro, watching their eyes meet, turned and headed in for a drink.

"Time for a beer."

The Cyclist's Tale

For a cyclist there are many different miles. Long winter miles in the cold and rain condition the legs and mind. Winding roads and country lanes of scented flowers cut deep into memory. Miles are whittled away during long hours of training. A few are fixed in the race of truth, when each mile is eked out against the clock, in a race over a fixed distance. Miles upon miles.

At times miles become kilometres. During bragging at the café. Fuzziness. A hundred: was it kilometres or miles?

For many, the miles are tallied. Intangible hours and distances are coded into notebooks or computers. Movement and efforts are fixed, forever. Distances accompany other numbers, heart rate and power. All to be compared and analysed. Tools to motivate and remember. Notes are included, the weather, the route. Proof, like a medal. I did this!

Big John liked keeping records. At the beginning of each ride he would mount his odometer, the latest bike computer, on his handlebars. It reassured him to look down at the numbers, check the effort. Could he go any harder? Was it a hard ride? How far had he been? Legs, mind and computer often disagreed.

His routine: doors locked, tyres checked, keys, money, sunglasses, helmet, mitts, energy drink, food, bike computer. Doors checked again and finally, riding. Even then, more checks, keys, money, food, and now heart rate, speed and distance.

Today he was going long. Setting out early, the

route already planned. Drinking and discussion of riders and clubs had pervaded the previous night. And always returned to how the Germans and Dutch felt they owned the road and couldn't be trusted. Rivalries. Them and us. The plan, thirty kilometres to the foothills, a break, and then the high mountains of Mallorca.

First steady from S'Arenal south of Palma, up the coast and heading inland along the lanes to Llucmayor. Then heading north, to Algaida, up the hidden valley. On to Sencelles via Pina. The roads were filled with cyclists, rolling through spring flowers. Some are training hard while others take it easy. In many groups the riders wear the same jersey. The towns are marked by churches on small rises. Finally, on to Inca, the second city, full of one−way streets. The last chance for a drink before the first climb of the day, the Col du Batala, just after Selva. Then the high mountains.

The first thirty kilometres kept much to plan.

John enjoyed fishing. Catching riders up ahead. A pair of small fry, an old couple out on rented bikes. A shark, full kit and a time trial bike. In each case John measured his effort slowly using the riders ahead to keep a steady pace and make progress. Sometimes, a group would roll past. John had been the fish.

John would then step up and hang on to the back of the bunch. Occasionally he'd help by riding at the front and doing some of the work. The shoal would eventually turn off and John would be on his own. He'd look up ahead for the next fish to catch. Gradually both miles and kilometres were covered.

The morning gives way to the heat of early afternoon and the start of the first big climb of the day, the Col du Batala. But first John stopped in Inca to refuel at a garage, with energy drinks and bars of chocolate. Escaping the one—way streets of the city, he followed other riders, they looked like they knew where they were going. He was soon on his way through Selva and at the bottom of the first climb.

Taking it steady, a few riders overtake, he holds his pace. 'Keep it steady,' it's going to be a long day. The switchbacks on the mountain keep coming. John monitors his figures. Heart rate, power, speed. A small group go past; 'let them go, John,' he mutters to himself under his breath. A little frustrated. His heart rate starts climbing. He finds it difficult, wanting to chase, to be the fastest on the road; to be the hunter.

More frustration, more riders pass, he looks down at the computer. The figures don't lie, he's laying down more power. 'How are they doing it? I'm better than this.'

At the next switchback he steps out of the saddle, another rider passes. Looking down, the figures show he's working almost at the limit. There is little more. His heart rate is maxed out. The figure for his power, the strength in his legs, is good. But not good enough, maybe, it's just not his day. He holds the wheel of the rider ahead; not too close. Just enough. Even more frustration. The rider ahead is pulling away. He looks heavier, bigger. Defying gravity. 'How the hell is he doing it?'

John keeps climbing. Three or more switchbacks ahead is the café at the top. Rest, a break, food and drink.

Sweat rolls down his arms, even more riders go past. He must be having a bad day. A few have similar jerseys. Dutch riders, they think they own the road. Maybe they do. They're killing him. Looking down again, his heart rate is high, he should be going faster, he can't. The last corner. The café.

After hooking the bike up, he removes the computer and heads into the café. A coffee: that will help. John orders a *café con leché* and an *ensaimada*, a local speciality. His frustration is getting the better of him. He'll just have to take it easy.

Many of the riders look hot, a few are laughing.

Most are recovering from the climb. The figures on his computer show the average speed, his heart rate, the power. Utter frustration. He's doing everything right, except he's going so slowly. If only he was a few years younger.

Fifteen minutes, that was enough. John had a long way to go and needed to get going. A quick nature break and back on the bike. Reassuringly John clicked the bike computer back into place. There was still a bit of a drag before the road started rolling. And then some more climbing. Somewhat refreshed, he started spinning up and increasing his pace. Looking out to the north–west, John could see the deep blues of the Mediterranean Sea and sky against the rocks and Cypress trees.

The road gently snaked, up and ahead. The pace felt good and no riders had passed. He felt much better, and could see a group of riders ahead. Steadily, he very gently raised the pace: he was reeling them in.

Orange jerseys. He looked down at the computer. His heart rate was steady, and speed was good. Maybe? He just might catch them at the top of the Sa Calobra exit. Left, straight down to the port with only one way out, straight back up the way you came. John was missing that today.

Sooner than expected, he was with the group with the orange jerseys. Sitting on the back, John sucked wheel, taking it a little easier. He looked along the line ahead, they were the Dutch riders that passed him earlier. They were working hard, with three or four riders rotating at the front. John decided he was going to go off the front in about a kilometre at the Sa Calobra exit. Until then he'd take it easy, he looked down, monitoring his heart rate.

Timing. A few hundred metres before the turn he started working his way up to the front. John's jersey marked him out as an outsider. He gave a slight nod as he passed every other rider. Almost there. Fifty metres, twenty–five, ten. John stepped up out of the saddle just as he went over the gravel at the turn.

Bang! John was off, he quickly ramped up the effort, turning his legs faster. Cranking the pedals hard, he distanced the group. He heard a bit of a shout, maybe a call, but it was too late. John was gone. Had he heard them say something about being English? Shit, they're not catching me. His head went down. Hands went to the drops. He measured his breathing. With the heat building up John unzipped his jersey and glanced behind.

Two riders had pulled away from the front of the pack and seemed to be trying to keep up. No way! John started pushing hard, and brushed the sweat off his face. His lungs, giant bellows, pumped the air in and out, fuelled the fire of his muscles. Again John looked back, they were still coming. Maybe they were getting closer. It looked like they were working together. Taking turns at cutting the air. That made it worse. Now he had to keep going. Where was the end, how long could he keep this up? John's mind blanked, as all that mattered was getting the air in and keeping the legs turning.

The road rolled along the mountain tops. John could do rolling, keeping the bike moving smoothly, topping up energy into the wheels. Weight didn't matter now. In fact, it started to work to his advantage. He looked back again, the orange shirts caught the sunlight. They were still there, chasing him down.

About four kilometres to the next climb, then he'd lose his advantage. The orange jerseys would sail past him. He'd be caught. No, not yet. Not if he could break their efforts. John thought he could hear their voices on the wind. Shit, he could hear his own heart in his ears. His legs were strong, but he knew he couldn't keep it going for much longer.

Another kilometre, road markers showed the distances down to Soller and Palma. Soon they would be passing the high lakes on the left. One year, John had watched helicopters picking up water to douse fires caused by the summer heat. When was that? Two, three years ago? It was hot. Now he had completely unzipped his jersey. He was flying now. In the zone. Totally focussed. John's eyes watched the road ahead, looking for every advantage. Carefully he picked his line, looking for the smooth tarmac. It made a difference. He looked back again.

John couldn't believe his eyes. One of the riders had been dropped. Elation. Still, the other rider was getting closer. Maybe. He glimpsed the effort, the position the Dutch rider was on the drops. Head down. Absolute determination.

John could match that. For a while. A change of gear, his muscles adapt, relaxing and then tensioning as John's legs turn at a new cadence, faster and smoother.

Drink. He must remember to drink, to stay fuelled. He grabbed at the bottle, gasping as he took sips between breaths. Why the hell was he doing this? That's what happens. New messages from the subconscious start popping up, calling the body to slow down, conserve energy. No. John knew the signs. Next it would be the legs. They would be shouting soon, calling him to stop.

Two kilometres now. If only he could break the guy. 'Keep going, I can do this, I am doing this.' His legs powered on, they were complaining now. Not too bad, it would get worse. Shit. Another look back. The guy was closing. He could start to make out patterns on the jersey.

Arghhhh, he pushed on, not giving up. He was not going to break, not before the climb, this was his road. Today he was the king. Sweat poured off him now, dripping from his face onto his legs. His eyes were sore, the salt irritated and burned. John brushed the sweat away from his forehead.

Just another kilometre to go before the tunnel.

From there on it would start to go uphill. John would make it to the tunnel. Looking back, the Dutch rider was closing in. Maybe a hundred metres or so behind. Less than a kilometre to go, he could do it. Just. His legs were burning now, calling. Shut up legs.

John thought he could hear a voice? No way. The Dutch rider was less than fifty metres now. There were just a few hundred metres to the tunnel. The entrance loomed up ahead. Now he could hear the rider's breathing. His own chest was heaving, Sweat dripped from his arms, face and legs. John couldn't make any more effort. He could hear the deep intakes of breath of the rider behind. It punctuated his own gasps as he struggled to fill the bellows.

The rider behind was now shouting, saying something, he couldn't quite make it out. John was almost at the tunnel.

His lungs heaving, the Dutch rider was struggling to get the words out. John could do no more, he was spent, the tunnel just a few metres away. Slowing, the Dutch rider came along side.

"Hello, are you Engleesh?"

They came to a stop. Both struggled for breath. The Dutch rider was tall, lean, his face narrow, his eyes bright blue. Glistening with sweat, he leaned over, there was something in his hand. Catching his breath:

"Are you English?" John nodded. The Dutch rider held out his hand.

"You have dropped your computer."

John wasn't sure, but there in front of him, where the bike computer should have been on the bars, was a space. Astonishment, disbelief, amusement, laughter. He hadn't noticed. At no point had he looked down for the numbers, his heart rate, his power. None of it had mattered.

This Dutch rider, what a rider! John must have dropped the computer at the turn off for Sa Calobra on the gravel, when he set off. Five kilometres ago.

Taking the computer, he clicked it into place and turned to the Dutch rider.

"Thank you!" John couldn't stop himself grinning and patted the Dutch guy on the back

"Thank you." There weren't any words that could match the effort the rider had made to return the computer.

"I am really grateful. I can't believe you did that!". The Dutch rider smiled while zipping up his jersey. They were both cooling down now. Turning around, without any more words, the rider rode back, to join up with his team mates.

Big John headed on through the tunnel. The computer, back in its place, held the story of the chase stored in its memory. Maybe the Dutch did own the roads. The bike computer was the latest and most expensive. John steadily pedalled on. There was a long way to go. Maybe a story for the bar? No, they wouldn't believe it.

The Vélo

$\mathbf{A}$ cycling club has history. History that is made on the road. In 1888, the bicycle, freeing people from the horse, was officially given the status of a carriage with the right to ride the highway. Some of the earliest clubs from the 1860's and 1870's still head out for their Sunday ride.

Club histories are long, with heroes and villains, challenges, meetings, agendas, trophies and medals. There are club legends, the remembered, memorial rides, politics and rivalries. All flow from love and passion. There is the bread and butter; the club runs, the chain gang, the club time−trial. And also the track night, the open fifty and now the sportive. Club names, once a subject on agenda and minutes, are now etched on trophies. Vivid jerseys proudly display club names, colours, and sponsors.

Joining a cycle club may be an easy decision. Especially when generations of families ride together. But considerations have to be made. What's the club's focus? Touring, Audax, racing, or track?

Davy's filled application form for the Wheelers lay on the table. He could have chosen the local Vélo or even the waning Clarion with its lost call. But, new to the town, it wasn't a difficult decision. The Wheelers had a race pedigree. Their results were good, both locally and nationally. Joining the weekly chain gang sealed his choice. He'd worked hard with each rider taking time on the front, cutting the wind. Being dropped on the last lap was better than expected. The ride was smooth, signals understood, experienced riders rotated front to back, making the right effort at the right time. Davy felt good, being back on the bike, being part of something. He needed a club.

There were riders who could spend hours on their own. Who knew how they stayed motivated? How could they work hard without somebody breathing down their neck or sucking wheel? But they were there, on the roads. Some were even members of a club. Davy needed company, the routine. It helped his motivation. Especially on the bad days. Cold and rain were good excuses if he was on his own. But in a club, you just couldn't let anybody down.

It was too late in the season to get any results, or even try. But he could start building up base miles. Start preparing for next year. The cycling year follows the season. Autumn and winter are where the real work is done. Building endurance. A race can be long with hour upon hour of riding, only to be lost on a single climb or crosswind breaking the peleton. Spring is where the power is honed, with interval training and early races. Cycle camps are attended, maybe Mallorca or Tenerife. The Spring Classics are the target if you're a pro. For the club racer it's steady work to build form and fitness.

Davy found the Wheelers to be an honest club, without too much politics. The late summer riding helped him pick up form. The miles started to increase. He'd quickly made friends with a few of the other members: Dubrowski, an old pro. There was Garvey, the club champion, and Mac who could take anybody on on a climb, including Garvey. They had started to train together, putting in the hours. It was on one of these rides that they passed a rider out training on his own.

Davy had started to recognise the local riders and had seen this guy before, out training, always on his own. The rider was *head down*, working like a dog.

Who was he? He rode over and asked Garvey.

"Who's the guy?"

"Ask Mac." Garvey looked uncomfortable and so Davy dropped back, side—by—side with Mac.

"Is he any good?" Davy pointed to the rider now some way in the distance.

"He was." Mac seemed agitated, but carried on.

"It's Tom, he always rides with the Vélo."

Mac put his head down, pushed up to the front and started to wind up the pace. Remembering back to when he'd joined the Wheelers, Davy had considered the Vélo. They had a low profile and only a few riders. The club had seen better days.

The late season has a rhythm unlike the rest of the year; the big races had been won or lost. Club competitions were rounding off. The madness of the cyclo—cross season was coming, along with the even crazier hill climbs.

Cyclo—cross really was madness. Why would you

want to carry your bike around the course? The idea of hopping on and off to negotiate fences, climbs and mud, and then go round again. No.

That left the hill climbs. He hadn't raced all season, but had picked up some late form and even started to match Garvey and Mac on the climbs. On a good day he had gone past them both.

It was something. Something to aim for. The club hill climb up the Pike was six weeks away. Late October. Time enough. He'd been up the Pike, way behind Garvey and Mac. Only Dubrowski was further behind. It was a tough climb, going up for just seven hundred and fifty metres. It had an average gradient of twelve percent, topping out at twenty−two percent for a few metres. There was even a hand rail for walkers. The club record had stood for thirty years, one minute and forty−two seconds. A good rider took more than three minutes.

The race itself was indeed crazy. Just seven

hundred and fifty metres, bottom to top. You just went as hard as you could, to the utter limit. At the top you had a catcher. You were totally spent. Exhausted. Legs and chest burned. In just a couple of minutes you were in complete agony. Without the catcher you'd fall off.

He'd brought the idea up on the Tuesday night ride. Dubrowski had rolled his eyes upwards. Garvey looked thoughtful. Mac, who normally would out−climb them all, gave Garvey a nod. After a short while Garvey spoke.

"It's a good choice. You'll be up against Tom and the Vélo. It's a joint club race."

Tom had always ridden with the Vélo, it was a family affair. His great, great, granddad had been a member in the 1870's. He'd ridden with his son, dad, granddad and nephews. His son, Luke, had been really coming on, winning some of his youth races. The Vélo rides were mostly leisurely, but Tom would keep the pace high on long and hard rides, while holding an eye on the road.

Tom didn't have time for the heavy training needed for the elite races. But there was always the club Hill Climb. Tom had won it every year since 2006. Once he'd almost touched the record. Down by seven seconds; it may as well have been seven hours. Tom had collapsed at the end. Thank goodness for the catchers.

Back with the Wheelers, Garvey was helping Davy with some interval training for the club Hill Climb. Garvey seemed pleased and said it was a good idea. Davy had signed up and started routinely going up the Pike, he'd soon know every inch. In a Hill Climb race every second is hard fought.

Davy started preparing his bike. Stripping it down to the bones. Six point eight kilos, no lighter. He'd also started losing weight. Usually he carried about seven percent body fat. That had to go. It was soon out there. A few of the other club members had commented.

"You're up against Tom and the Vélo?" Always a question and statement, with a distant look on their faces. There was something he wasn't seeing. It wasn't long now. Only two weeks away. Since 2006, the club Hill Climb had always been on the last Sunday in October.

During the final week, he started getting nervous. It seemed it was a big event. Bigger than he'd expected. He hadn't seen the list of starters but knew Tom would be riding. People around town gave him the nod. The club had even put bunting up the Pike on the eve of the race.

Davy had trained hard and felt in great form, he'd make a good effort. So far, the best he'd done was two minutes and five seconds. Way off the record. That was without a catcher, and he had more to give. Racing was about preparation and Davy felt prepared.

On the morning of the race, Davy was up early

having slept poorly. It wasn't really a problem, the race would be over in just a few minutes! Each rider setting off on their own. A two minute or so time trial up seven hundred and fifty metres of agonising hell. Ready or not, it would soon all be over.

Davy cycled over to the bottom of the Pike. The Pike was packed with spectators, three deep all the way to the top. All ready to urge him up, to give everything. With pulse raised, he could feel the tension.

As matter of routine, he walked over to the entry desk for signing on. When did he start? Who was racing? Who was he up against? The guys were there waiting: Garvey, Mac and Dubrowski.

Garvey punched him in the arm.

"Ready?" It was a question and statement.

Looking down at the entry list he could see just two names. Just two! Tom and himself. Was this true? To Garvey:

"Just Tom and me?" Garvey looked up at the Banner across road at the bottom of the Pike and smiled gently and replied

"Sure, just you and the Vélo!"

THE 2006 VÉLO MEMORIAL HILL CLIMB

Tom arrived a few minutes later to a big cheer from the crowd. Tom's bike, like his own, was pared down to the bare bones. Tom looked emaciated skin, tendon, bones and muscle. Tom was ready.

The crowds were here for just a few minutes of racing. It was hard to make sense of the faces. The spectators watched intensely. They were apprehensive and waiting quietly.

A coin toss. Davy was going first, Tom was to follow. They had twenty minutes to warm up on the rollers.

It was soon over. Tom was next. Davy could

remember setting off and the first few metres. The rest was a blur. The pain was already gone, he'd tried to give everything. But when Davy arrived at the finish line, the catchers just looked at him, he didn't need their help.

Davy unclipped and set his bike against the stone wall, just beyond the finish line. He remembered the crowd cheering and clapping, maybe a little subdued. There had been big applause as he passed the finish line, just before the cattle grid. A fleeting image of a stony face flashed into his mind. There was something more to this race. He waited for Tom.

Tom took his place on the line, the spectators quiet. Tom looked at the time on his watch: ten fifteen, the last Sunday in October. Trembling and shaking, those close could see the tears in Tom's eyes. Tom was clipped in. A marshal was holding Tom and his bike and the time keeper was counting down. Deep down, Tom was somewhere else.

The morning was cold. The Vélo met up at the Waltzing Weasel car park. They all lined up in winter longs with jackets and gloves. There had been a frost. It was definitely a day for winter training bikes, with mudguards and wide tyres. Tom had decided on the route: main roads, gritted. They weren't going to take any risks. Soon the Vélo were moving through the crisp coastal air. Tom with his son Luke, his dad, granddad and Joe. They kept a steady pace. Tom leading as usual.

Just as they headed up the first drag of the day, the car came rolling over the top. Not rolling. Sliding. At the apex, all four wheels lost grip. With a slight reverse camber at the top, the car crossed the carriageway. For the Vélo, there was no place to go. They were simply skittles waiting to be knocked down. By the time the car had come to a stop, a boy and three men lay dead in the road, with bikes crushed. Utter carnage. Tom had been thrown off his bike, over the wall. His leg and wrist mangled, broken. Next to him, just on the other side of the wall lay his son Luke, dead.

A passing car stopped and made the first call. Ambulance and police, blue lights flashing. Four dead. Joe had been crushed into the wall. Luke had been the first, his neck broken: Dad and Granddad both died with multiple injuries, bones crushed and broken. The bikes lay lifeless, mangled, across both carriageways like carcasses. The driver, bruised, gripped the steering wheel. Shock.

The marshal raised his voice.

"Three, two, one." Fingers indicating the remaining seconds, disappeared one by one. The marshal shouted encouragement.

"Go. Go Tom, go."

The crowd erupted. Every spectator knew. Tom was there for his son, his family, the Vélo. Their voices, a wall of sound, carried Tom up the Pike. Tom exploded upwards with everything he had. Tom, now riding with the Vélo. His legs on fire. Deep down he could feel Luke behind him, His Dad just up ahead. Joe and Granddad were behind Luke. They all were calling:

"Go on Tom, you can do it."

Cold air filled Tom's lungs. His heart beat as fast as it could. Swinging up the first section, he remembered the silence of that morning in 2006. And now, the Pike was exploding around him, willing him upwards. Luke, Joe, Dad and Granddad, they were there with him. The shouts of the crowd filled his mind.

"Go on Tom. Push. Go." Tom pushed and pulled at the pedals as hard as he could.

Now it was getting steep. Really steep. He pushed the bike over side−to−side to get more leverage and pulled on the bars. Only two hundred and fifty metres to go.

Two hundred and fifty. Time slows, eyes are becoming bloodshot. Each pedal stroke forcing more fuel to be burned. Anaerobic now, muscles are starting to destroy themselves, they can't keep it going. The brain ignores the pain — keep going. Another hundred metres are gone. The road eases, the pain increases. The lungs are bursting.

Collapse feels imminent. Fifty metres to go. The Vélo start pushing, he hears Luke, Joe, Dad and Granddad — they're shouting now — one last effort. Ten metres, five. The line. Collapse. The waiting arms of the catcher. Nothingness. Davy watched on, he had been well beaten.

Tom didn't beat the record that day. He was close again. Just three seconds away. It had felt hard, Tom could do no more. The will of the crowd helped him overcome the pain. Without the Vélo he couldn't do it. Tom had flown up the Pike like a bird. The club record still stood. It had taken a few moments for the time keepers to confer. They checked and double checked. Each time keeper had two watches. They nodded. The results spread up the Pike. There was a slight gasp, Tom was so close. Then a thunderous cheer and clapping rose up the Pike. Full of warmth and love.

For those that know the Pike, a large rock, a faded mile marker marks the start of the Hill Climb, just past the gate on the left. The finish is a metre before the cattle grid at the top. Walkers pass by without giving these landmarks a second thought.

Footnote: This story is a tribute to the Rhyl Cycling Club. In August 2006, 12 riders set out on their Sunday club run. Only 8 returned. Three men and a young boy of 14 were killed in Britain's worst ever bike accident. At Abergele a car hit black ice and lost control. The Police had asked Conwy County Council to grit the road following an accident at the same spot an hour earlier. The driver was later fined for having three bald tyres. Although not considered to be factor in the accident, many felt that the driver was going too fast for the conditions, and were disappointed he wasn't prosecuted for dangerous driving. Rhyl cycling club still rides today.

Wheels Within Wheels

Big John had been working for twenty−three seconds. The target for the club ten had been nineteen minutes and forty−one seconds, the club record. For the last two years he'd used the numbers for his credit card. He was getting close. Twenty−three seconds close.

Time on a bike is many things. An ally, a friend, a passenger, an enemy. Sometimes an absolute, a reference. Often a vagary. Moments slow to a freeze frame. Seconds, minutes, hours and even years are lost to the walls of the mind. A time trial is the *Race of Truth*. Big John could do time trials, they were in his blood. A fixed distance as fast as you could go. No drafting, no help, no peleton. Just the rider, the bike, the course.

The history of the time trial is long. In England when the racing of bicycles was banned, riders could be seen setting off early on Sunday mornings to race against the clock. Courses are still laid out in handbooks. Strange numbers codify the routes. Start points are numbers on telegraph poles, ends at gate posts and signs. Riders at cafés become code breakers, 'Last week I cracked the J21 course.'

Courses are hard, and easy. Circular, or out and back. Fast and slow. Records are held by the greats and anonymous alike. There are events at all levels. Club, national and international – the World's. The Race of Truth can even hold the key to winning the grand tours, the Giro, the Vuelta and, of course, the Tour de France. Races that are hard fought over thousands of miles can be settled in a time trial, by a few awkward seconds. Of course you probably know this.

So far it had been a good race for Big John. The course, hard and circular, was considered slow. He'd made sure his bike was set up to perfection. His set−off was smooth. As the time keeper started the stopwatch, John immediately laid the power down, watt after watt. At each corner the marshals waved him through, no traffic, a clear ride. No wind to help and none to fight. Early evening, everything had been right. On setting off he'd started his bike computer, the briefest of touches on his handle bar. Today was going to be *the day.*

Tom was responsible for the Wheelers time keepers, the two stopwatches used for the time trials. Each year he would send them away to be serviced and calibrated. Tom took the responsibility very seriously despite only being an honorary member of the Wheelers. Tom's main club had always been the Vélo. And the Vélo hadn't organized any time trials for a few years. So Tom would help the Wheelers out and occasionally act as a marshal for the local ten mile time trial. The club ten.

The job had fallen to Tom as he had a small watch repair shop in the high street. Just like many things, watches follow fashions. Since the seventies, quartz watches had become cheap and cheerful. A battery and a silicon chip measured the time of a vibrating crystal. But now people were longing for the simpler days. Days when a watch had to be wound, when it ticked. There had been a renaissance in hand made watches. It fitted Tom well.

Tom found that working on the minute mechanisms transported him to another place just like cycling. There was beauty in the fine mechanical parts, the precision of the little wheels and pinions as they worked together to measure time.

His shop was busy, passers—by were drawn into the mechanical microcosm. At the front window was a display of his finest time pieces. A large magnifying glass was positioned over one so the parts could be seen moving. All the little wheels driving each other, alive, measuring time.

For many in the town it was a routine. Stopping for a moment, they checked their own watches, sometimes making an adjustment. They would gaze, and look at the promise of perfection in the little mechanical machines. Tom took great pride in checking these mechanical masterpieces, and each day he would make sure they were accurately set.

Now for Big John the time trial was going well. The first stretch was tricky, with a bit of rough road and gravel. But soon after, he was in his stride. He arrived at the first left turn, his pace was comfortable, his breathing deep, regular and easy, his legs were strong. The trick was to measure the effort. To make each stroke of the pedal count. To be smooth with no unwanted movement, to be a machine. As he cranked the pedals he could hear the sound of the wheels, a beautiful whoosh, whoosh, whoosh. This was fast, he was fast. He could already see his minute man up ahead, the rider that had been set off just one minute before him. He would catch him soon.

Big John was on the longest stretch, he had overtaken the minute man a while back and could see the next left hander ahead. The marshal was already indicating the turn was clear. Braking just at the right time, he turned a little, then gravel, and on the power again. Now he raced by hedgerows, picking the smoothest surfaces. A sense of knowing. His form was good. Looking down at his bike computer, he could see he was approaching half way.

Each morning, Dubrowski stopped at Tom's window on his way to the plant, it was one of the last factories still in the town. He knew Tom rode with the Vélo. Dubrowski, an old pro cyclist, now worked as a factory caretaker. Dubrowski also looked after some of the simpler machines and each day he would sound the horn for the morning shift. He appreciated Tom's watches and found himself, like many, drawn into the microscopic world in the window. After a short while he would set his watch and be on his way.

Half way. Now for the pain. Big John's breathing was on the edge, his mouth was dry. It took just that little bit more effort to keep a smooth style. He held a neat tuck on the aero bars. Part of the skill was keeping that position: compact, drag—reducing. Now the slight incline, here it would hurt, his weight counted against him. It wasn't much but he could feel it. Was that his two minute man? It was. Just as he came around the next bend he could see him ahead. It was Garvey! Surely he hadn't made up that amount of time. But there he was, he was reeling Garvey in. One for the books. Whatever the outcome.

Big John was lifted, despite the pain. He tried to stop himself working too hard to catch Garvey, he still had a couple of miles to go. He didn't want to crack. Slowly he came up on Garvey. Without a nod, he passed, he could feel the strength in his legs. Today he was on form. The computer showed his heart rate, just above threshold. He eased off, the slightest of touches, and still he pulled away from Garvey. The road started to roll now, for the last few miles.

That week, Tom had noticed that each morning, Dubrowski would stop and look in the window. He would spend quite a while looking at all the watches. Tom, like most, knew that Dubrowski rode with the Wheelers. Dubrowski was a small quiet man about ten years or so older than most of the riders in the club. They'd both been out together a few times, but never really talked. Tom knew Dubrowski was an ex pro but other than that, little else.

Shit. Just as Big John came round the last bend a tractor had pulled out. There was just room. A hard decision. He overtook. It was dangerous and tight, he'd have to make even more effort, just to stay ahead. His legs were burning. He was struggling to breathe. There was no giving in. Not now, not today.

Big John looked down at the figures. The slightest of moves, keeping the tuck neat, the pedals smooth. It looked good, he knew this was his fastest, by far. The course record dangled in front of him. Surely, he dare not think that far. So close. He could still crack. Now his legs were screaming. The blood in his ears pounded, still John kept the pedalling smooth.

Thoughts flooded in, when should he start the sprint? Every second counted. Conflict. Was that a cramp? Every muscle, ache and pain monitored. His eyes were glued on the road a few metres ahead. Big John still hunted for the smoothest surface. Dare he look behind? No. Garvey was long gone, maybe cracked. Somebody passing will do that to the mind, the body follows, waiting for any excuse to give up. He only had to beat the record by one second, one was enough. His bank card numbers are in his mind. One, nine, four, one. Nineteen minutes and forty−one seconds. He could do it, he was doing it.

Time plays tricks on a bike as seconds become minutes. John knew this. The mind races as the body demands an end to the punishment. But time can be squeezed, cajoled, put back in the box. Today is the day for the record. There are few days like this and Big John only had half a mile to go.

Still smooth and in the tuck Big John can see the race marshals up ahead. The time keepers sit on chairs with a clipboard and stopwatch in their hands. Now just a third of a mile. He can see the tree he sprinted from last time. Then he'd gone too early and died a few metres from the line. John waited and cranked the pedals. His calf muscles and thighs were on fire. His lungs heave.

Soon it would be over. Maybe too soon. John passed the tree and counted his breaths. Pulling and pushing, he leaves the saddle. The bike is swinging under him as he sprints. Each muscle fibre is giving everything and burning itself up to propel him across the line. John remembers. He presses the button on his computer. The coughing starts, his lungs and throat are dry. He could do no more.

The bike rolled to a stop, and John fell forward resting his head on the bars. That was a big effort. He looked down at the numbers and smiled.

It's always much the same. Big John waited in the Waltzing Weasels car park. His throat was still dry, he was still coughing. It would be a while before it eased and he could breathe easily. A few bikes were already loaded back into cars. There were just a few late starters to get back.

Garvey rode in, he didn't look good, maybe it was a bad day. That happens. It was now a question of waiting for the list. A few scribbles on a clipboard. The evidence. The truth. Big John had already seen his time on his handlebars. It was a very good day. Garvey came over.

"A drink? John, you were really going some!"

Any day was a good day he could get past Garvey, Big John was happy.

"Sure, I think I earned it today. That was hard work."

Tom and one of the other marshals and time keepers had just entered the car park with the infamous clipboard. They had the results.

A huddle soon materialised. Murmurs. A few raised voices and some sighs. Riders started coming away. Emotions were mixed and spread across their faces. Disappointment, relief, some were pleased, others were blank, still white after the effort. The numbers are shared, compared, considered. Expectations may be dashed. Thoughts whirl, words are muttered under breath. 'Surely I had done better?'.

Big John had held back, he caught Tom's eye and

finally headed over. The huddle was gone. Tom had a big beaming smile.

"A great ride John, this year's record!"

Big John looked down at the numbers, there it was: nineteen minutes and forty four seconds. Big Johns face was blank. Emotionless. He tried to hide his disappointment.

"You almost had the club record." Tom put his hand on his John's shoulder. "Well done."

So he'd missed the club record by three seconds. Three seconds? His stomach felt queasy. Passing Garvey.

"Garvey, I definitely need a drink, are you ready?"

Locking up the bike, he removed the computer from the handle bars and looked at the numbers. Again. Nineteen minutes and thirty nine seconds. Two seconds faster than the club record. Two. Two whole seconds. Big John switched the little machine off and, quietly putting it in his pocket, headed in for a drink.

Dubrowski and Garvey were already at the bar with drinks in their hands. Garvey passed a pint to Big John.

"Your usual John. That was a great ride."

"Garvey tells me you sailed past him!" Dubrowski, who was in his civvies, hadn't ridden. Garvey and Dubrowski raised their glasses to John's ride.

"You only missed the record by three seconds." They both could see the disappointment on Big John's Face.

"Yeh, but what a great ride. Awesome. Another day you'd have had it in the bag!"

The conversation went on. Then there was the usual pattern. They ordered food and started discussing bikes, rides, the club meeting, results, training and sometimes work.

Big John couldn't stop himself reflecting on his

time. He remembered starting his clock just as he set off and stopping it just after he passed the finish line.

Dubrowski, the old pro, catches Tom's eye at the bar and waves him over.

"Hey Tom, we were just talking about the accuracy of the stop watches." They weren't. Big John's eyes widened. Dubrowski continued.

"How accurate are the stop watches?" Tom answered confidently.

"We send them away twice a year for checking. They're accurate to a tenth of a second and read to the hundredth." Tom carried on.

"I also check them once a week against my own watches."

Dubrowski smiled, lightly.

"I guessed as much. I was outside your shop this morning. You've got some great watches there, how do you keep them so accurate?"

Tom looked up from his drink.

"It's not too difficult. Each morning I check the watches, most are okay. A few are off by a few seconds and need adjusting. I use the morning shift horn from the plant. You can just about hear it from my shop."

Dubrowski smiled, he remembered setting his watch that morning at Tom's shop, He'd cycled over to the plant and without a thought looked down at his watch and as the second hand hit the hour, at eight thirty, Dubrowski sounded the horn. Just as he did every morning. Dubrowski looked at Tom and smiled.

"Good to know."

Then nodded to Big John.

"Not to worry John, there's always a next time!"

Emily sat at the desk looking at the numbers. They meant nothing to her, it was all automated. She'd been watching, babysitting the consoles, at the bunker for six months. It would soon be the end of her tour. Join the United States Army. Emily dimly remembered the recruitment advert promising action and adventure. She looked at the numbers and then the clocks. There were five. Five atomic clocks. Each with a precision of a second in hundreds of thousands of years. Yet one was not enough. The average of the five was the reference. The master time.

Signals stretched up from the bunker to the global position system satellites. Each satellite had three atomic clocks. The Army was tasked with the keys to the system. Clocks had to be set. Three times in every twenty four hours, each of the three clocks on each satellite had to be corrected. Each satellite then transmitted the average of these clocks as a global position system reference.

A global position system system needs at least four satellite time references to get an accurate position. The reading enables triangulation using simple geometry. Any position on planet earth can be found to within a few metres. So each of the satellite's atomic clocks has to be corrected three times a day, to account for the micro-changes in time from Einsteinian Relativity. The clocks change as a result of movement, mass, and their place in the Universe.

So that time, that day, that ride, the time measured on Big John's bike computer was the result of at least seventeen atomic clocks working together. Three in each satellite and five in the United States Army bunker. Big John knew this and guessed he probably had broken the course record. Time. So it goes.

The Budgie and the Clerk

He looked up at the television. There, kept safe by his team, in the midst of the peleton, was his old friend.

The television screen was full of brightly coloured cyclists racing through fields of sunflowers. Motorbike outriders with precariously balanced cameramen followed the bunch. Helicopters shadowed overhead and relayed the live camera feed to the world. The road was alive with movement.

Well, maybe not a friend, more of a team mate. They had raced together in the local youth team on the track, at the velodrome. He watched the screen. A team rider, a *domestique*, had been sent back to the car for water, and now passed biddons out. The riders tossed the empties to the roadside, fans grabbed the bottles for a keepsake. The commentator was enthusiastically explaining that his old team mate was doing well and could even win the Tour.

Joe was doing well. Very well, he was winning in the local youth individual challenge cup. Joe's Dad would bring him to the velodrome and stand against the track rail, shouting encouragement. Joe and Davy trained together; Davy had started riding with the school and, after a few sessions, had really taken to it. Davy went a few times a week, it was good fun and an escape from his grandma's flat. There were also a few other locals, friends of Davy, who were regulars at the track and members of the youth team. They had some really good riders, like Joe.

The Velodrome was magnificent. Only a few

years before, it had been wasteland. It was just a mile or so from the flat, where Davy lived with his grandma. At first, Davy had borrowed a bike from the Velodrome. Then his grandma lent him some money to buy a track bike, a bike with a fixed gear and no freewheel. It was second hand, beaten up and needed a bit of work. It did the job.

Meanwhile Joe's newest bike had the latest carbon wheels. Davy had ridden it, but Joe's dad hadn't been happy about that; so it had just been for a lap or two. Now that was a great bike.

Most of the racing was on Wednesday night with the youth league. Joe and Davy's team were at the top of the table. Their coach was an ex national rider and had helped. A lot. Although most of Joe's coaching appeared to be done by his dad. Joe's dad would stand track—side, with the other mums and dads, shouting instructions and support.

Davy enjoyed the riding, it was good fun. Every

now and then he'd have a good night and do okay, but mostly Joe would win. This year it looked like Joe was going to win the youth challenge cup, he was unstoppable. For Davy, his old bike was a godsend. It meant he could skip school. He could get out and within an hour be in the city. Nobody would bother him, he was just another kid skipping school. His gran didn't get out much from the flat. Her highlight of the week was the visit to the bingo hall. Davy would help with the shopping and other chores.

The television was showing today's stage of the Tour. It was long and flat. The commentator was explaining it that was a day for the sprinters. For the race's main contenders, the team's job was to keep their leader safe and to get them to the mountains.

There was a lot of anxiety in the peleton. The riders were keeping an eye out for splits in the bunch. The route along the coast was difficult at this time of year. Strong winds could divide the peleton. If you were the wrong side of the spilt, you could lose minutes. Once there was a split, it was hard to get the bunch back together. The wind creates an impenetrable wall for even the strongest rider.

A Tour could be lost to the wind on just a single day. The riders were edgy, and started to form echelons, diagonal lines across the road as riders tried to shelter from the winds and protect their leaders. It looked sketchy out there.

As a result, the breakaway was being reeled in quicker than expected. The breakaway, a small group of riders, had been left dangling up front for almost a hundred kilometres and were now struggling with the headwinds. There was no point in the bunch catching the breakaway too early. The peleton acted as a single organism, and could quickly raise the pace, and pick them up — when they needed to. The word was usually given over the race radio, to get a move on and make the catch. It was good for the cameras and sponsors having the breakaway out front. If the peleton timed it right, they would catch the carrots in the last few hundred metres. It made exciting watching for the television.

Once in a while, the peleton would get it wrong and fail to catch the breakaway. The sprinters would lose their chance and be left flapping and sprinting for third or fourth for the crowd. Then the day's race would be won by a minor rider or domestique, who'd have a great story to tell their grandchildren. Today, the sprinters teams' job was to make sure that didn't happen, they would work against the wind to give their man his chance. Their sprinter would be sitting in the bunch, saving energy for the last few moments.

At the Velodrome the youth team would practice sprinting. It was hard on a track bike. With a single fixed gear, you had to keep the pedalling smooth. That was a real challenge, few could do it well. Sprinting was a game of poker, you had to time it just right and then give it everything. Surprise helped. Get your position right and you won. Get it wrong and go too early and you'd help the rider sitting behind on your wheel. They'd be waiting to sail by in the last second.

He remembered their very first practice sprint and the coach putting up the results. Fractions of seconds split the whole group, he'd been a good sprinter.

Looking up at the television he could see something had happened. The commentator was getting excited. One of the main general classification contenders had stopped with a mechanical. His chain had come off. This was a dangerous time. A team mate had given him his own bike and was now waiting for a replacement from the team car. The team leader needed pacing back to the peleton. That was going to be hard in these winds. Maybe not, the message had gone to the front. Sportsmanship. The peleton, controlled by the main contenders, had lowered the pace so the rider with the mechanical could get back on. Messages travelled back and forth on the team radio. It wasn't sporting to attack a rival with a mechanical. The commentator explained it all.

Rules seemed to be made up on the road and were strangely esoteric. The rider with the mechanical was being led back by a couple of team mates. They were drafting team cars to move back up the field. Soon, the peleton would be all back together. Drafting the cars was illegal, but the judges would let it slide. The race had to be fair, and they needed the elite riders to be battling it out on the mountains — for the viewing figures.

To the outsider, or the uninitiated, a bicycle race is unfathomable. It's just a bunch of riders cycling up the road. Something is going on and people seem to be excited, but what is happening? Who knows? But for those that follow the Tour, it is the Greatest Show on Earth. It's not just a few hours on a Saturday afternoon. It's twenty—one days of beauty. An endurance event that includes thousands of miles, the highest mountains, strategy and luck. And each minute can change the course of the twenty—one day race.

Each day is a new stage with a new winner for that day, while the main contenders, the general classification guys, bide their time, protected by their team mates. They wait, their team works for them. They are waiting for the chance to gain time on their rivals. The yellow jersey holds the race lead with the shortest overall time.

The Tour, over thousands of miles, has been won on seconds. There are allegiances, strategy, rivalries, epic efforts. There are casualties, chances lost and taken. Each summer, for twenty—one days of the Tour de France, millions of viewers watch on the edges of their seats. For many, it just passes them by.

The coach had told everyone that the national pro team scout was going to be at the Wednesday youth league track meeting. There were more Dads at the race track than usual. They were all hoping their son or daughter would be selected, to be a neo—pro, an apprentice professional bicycle racer.

Joe's dad was in his usual spot and as proud as punch. Joe had almost won the league and was already a few points ahead. Joe's dad had even bought him a new bike for the occasion. The Velodrome, usually quite empty, buzzed with excitement. It was the last night of the season. Joe tried to make out the scout, it could be anybody. But you didn't need to be a scout to see that Joe was a great rider.

The points race was the showcase of the night. Joe had won most of the points races during the season. One hundred laps. Points are awarded for sprints every ten laps for the first four across the line. If you could do it, you could get twenty points for lapping the main field. It was a big ask. Joe's strategy had been to win the sprints and chase down anyone going for a lap. It had worked. But tonight the scout was here, so he was going for lap. It would be unexpected, a real show of strength.

For the first half of the race, Joe had come in second and third on the sprints, and slowly built up his tally. The field was nervous and the pace high. No one had even attempted a breakaway for a lap. That needed a few riders working together and, tonight, with the scout present, that wasn't going to happen.

Davy sat in the bunch, there was no point sprinting, he didn't have that edge. But there were some small signs, the way Joe was racing. Joe was sitting back, just a little, waiting. Davy could see it and started riding on Joe's wheel. At the half way point, Joe hadn't even gone for the last sprint. Maybe? Davy held tight to Joe's wheel and gathered his energy.

There it was, just after the lap sixty sprint. Almost immediately. Joe started pounding the pedals, Davy tucked in and went with him. His old bike groaning, Joe's carbon wheels whooshed ahead. Hold on! Davy gritted his teeth, the first half-lap killed him. He put in a short effort taking his turn to cut the air. They worked together, it would take a couple of circuits. Then, just as his legs were ready to give way, the main field was ahead. They had made the lap. Joe was struggling and breathing heavily. But coming up behind the main field, they had both done it. Twenty points.

The remaining laps went quickly. Joe defended his advantage chasing down anyone else trying to push ahead. Meanwhile, Davy sat in the pack, anonymously. He wouldn't make the podium but at least he had some points.

The scout had been asked to take a look at the lad who had, apparently, some potential. It was hard to tell and you could get it wrong, but mostly he could see it. After forty-two years working for professional teams, he could read the signs. The lad had won the league competition and done well tonight. The dads were there. Up against the rail, he wondered which one was the lad's dad? He'd have to deal with him.

Up on the television, the peleton had caught the breakaway with about twenty kilometres to go. There was still an open stretch and as they went through the crossroads, the wind picked up. A split in the peleton had formed. The sprinters teams were on the wrong side, they had been caught napping. Now they were frantically starting to try and bridge the gap.

Only one of the sprinters had made the split. Two of the yellow jersey contenders had made the cut and their teams had started pushing the pace up; they were trying to take time out of their rivals.

There was a lot of buzz on the race radio. The wind was a real problem, the sprinters wouldn't have their day. All hell had let loose and some of the teams weren't happy. A lot of riders were being shed off the back bunch.

So there he was on the couch watching this race. Joe remembered that night at the Track. He'd won the League Trophy. It still stood on the mantelpiece. That night his dad had told him he was going to be a neo-pro. He'd raced well and won the points race. Joe's dad had been furious when he found out. It wasn't long after that his dad stopped taking him to the Track.

That night all those years ago, the coach had chosen Davy. Little Davy! And there was Davy on the screen in front of him, thanking his team mates for keeping him safe. The day's stage had been won by the solitary sprinter that had just made the cut. Davy, having made the split, was still in the race for the yellow jersey and was now just a few seconds off the race lead.

Davy stepped into the coach, most of the team were already there. They all looked tired, it had been a hard day. He'd have to pay them back in the mountains. Then the race would really take off.

A couple of the race contenders who'd not made the cut were furious, and were pointing out that they'd held the peleton up for Davy's mechanical. How could Davy's team split the peleton so close to the finish? It wasn't sporting, was it? It was a sprinters' day, wasn't it? Davy had his instructions. Davy was going to win the Tour, to do what it takes, to do what was needed.

For the scout, it had been simple. He didn't just watch how they rode. There was more. It was how they held their bike, how they spoke to the other riders, the responses, the smiles, the balance. Pro cycling wasn't just about being on the bike, there was more to it. Much, much more. It was a job, a hard job, you had to enjoy it. The lad on the old bike had caught his eye, especially the way he'd followed Joe and taken the lap in the points race.

There was something about him, he could see it. The boy loved the bike and the velodrome. The bike was old, there was no dad on the rail. Davy hadn't been pushed or pulled, he just rode hard. Davy had the will, the physique, and he'd read the race. The lad had what it took. Passion. And that something else. Potential.

Joe looked up at the television. The commentators discussed the cyclists' style of riding. Apparently, one of the riders looked like a Victorian clerk, with his arms flapping. While the other looked more like a budgie, nodding on a perch. Joe smiled at the shot of the riders climbing. Joe could see it straight away. Flapping and pecking. It was quite funny.

Déjà vu

What a wonderful day, Jake's pace had been high. It was now mid—season. winter and spring training had paid off with great form and good results. Jake's favourite training loop rolled ahead through open moors and small villages. There was little traffic and only a light summer breeze. High up, streets of clouds stretched across a Mediterranean blue sky into the distant horizon.

The bike was running smoothly, so smooth; gently soaking up the road. Every effort, every watt of power eked from his muscles pushed him forward. His muscles felt fresh and full of wonderful form. Jake's breathing was comfortable and steady. The chain turned like silk. His wheels sang as they cut the air with a whisper, and the sun was warm on his back.

Even the ride out of town was good. A few drivers had waved him on with a warm smile. It was his fastest ride to date. Jake's effort felt easy, he was a boy again, with no worries, and no responsibilities. A lightness comes from the road. Knowing that you have the freedom to ride, the freedom to feel the wind and the sun. His body was singing in harmony with the bike and the road.

At the edge of town was the long drag before the rolling hills. Even that felt good. Jake had kept his pace even, monitoring his breathing and holding a steady rhythm. It felt like the wind was pushing him upwards, but today there was only the lightest of breezes. Maybe he would do the loop a couple of times?

The smell of cut grass brings back memories of his wife, their first meeting. They had met with the sparkle of youth in their eyes. It had been life at first sight, they'd both felt it, a life to share. Jake remembered the smell of cut grass mixed with her perfume, her essence. She filled his mind and is beside him. His focus is drawn back to the road. The road will soon be rolling through the open moors. Dry stone walls shelter him from the slightest of crosswinds. Next is the wall.

The road drops a little, after the drag. Enough so he can pick up speed for the climb through the village. It isn't long, maybe a kilometre. Half way, at the postbox, the road heads sharply up to form the wall. Jake picks up his speed, he steps out of the saddle. His legs feel good, really good. Today he is a climber. Like never before. The cranks turn smoothly. Seeing the end of the short climb, he keeps his focus. He is there.

Now the rolling roads. Sheep lazily eat grass

beside the stone wall. He passes the reservoir. With increasing pace he drops the chain to the smallest cog on the cassette, an eleven. And with a fifty three chain wheel at the front, he is thundering along. Jake sips a drink from his biddon. He is comfortable, his hands are on the drops.

More thoughts fill Jake's mind. The day his son was born. He pictures his son, in the arms of his wife at the hospital, and then graduating at Oxford. How quickly those years had passed. His son was doing well. Life had treated them all well. There had been problems, of course, they had overcome them. Together, they had stood against the harder times. But that was long ago.

For a few kilometres, the road rolls gently upwards. The rise slows him a little, but still he keeps the pace high. Usually there was the odd complaint from the knee. Jake remembered falling down stairs at home, in the house. How clumsy he'd been. His left knee still called him on cold days or after long hours on bike; it was silent today. Jake could feel the energy flow from his heart to his legs, then to the pedals and the road. There was no mutter from the shoulder, he'd broken it when riding on ice one February. How many years ago was that? No, his shoulder felt good, Jake felt good. He held his body low, his hands still on the drops. His cadence, the speed he spun the pedals, felt natural. Jake had trained hard to raise his cadence. Today it felt fast, it was right.

The road continues and now rolls downwards. Jake rides fast. Only the wind can slow him. A light breeze is behind, his cadence increases further. He paces himself, an open−topped car passes. He holds his speed, the driver is taking it easy on this lovely day. Slowly, the car drifts away. Jake maintains his pace, his breathing increases, still he is comfortable. The air feels soft and warm in his lungs. Memories of distant winter rides, of cold rain, and sharp air on the face, mirror the day's ride. The differences, the reflections, highlight the wonder of the day.

Soon it will be the fastest section, then a short climb into the next village. Before the climb the road drops again, there's a little bend. He needs to pick up speed to get up the climb, taking care to keep to his side of the road. Jake is careful. Today he is fast, the descent is really fast, his cadence is smooth. Knowing every bump in the road, every pot hole, Jake keeps his line perfect. Now the bend.

Déjà vu. He feels it as he passes the bend, his speed carries him up into the village. The feeling isn't uncomfortable, just something. Something intangible. The sense of being there before. This has happened before.

Of course it had, this was his favourite training loop. It was routine through autumn, winter, spring, and now summer. It was a route that flowed through the years. A gentle warmth fell across him as his mind settled into the ride. He'd pass through villages and towns as he made the loop back home.

The roads are narrow and fill his senses. Jake's mind drifts, as eyes focus on the road ahead. The hedgerows are deep green and full of the scent of flowers. Time moves quickly, there's a flow to his riding like never before. He feels light, the air fresh in his lungs, maybe a little dry. The tyres caress the road. Soon he is back at the beginning of his training loop. Today is great day, a day for a few repeats. It doesn't get any better than this.

And again. The road across the moors keeps rolling. The slight descent before the bend. Jake picks up speed and again picks his way through the bumps and pot holes. He pictured his wife in hospital with his son in her arms. He hears her calling him 'Jake, Jake can you hear me?' He remembers the wonderful sound of her voice. The softness. Jake's heart quickens a little, there is something coming in the other direction. He centres the bike in his lane. There it is again, Déjà vu, of course.

Jake had ridden this section, not forty minutes ago. Yet it felt strange. Unworldly. This had happened before, there was something. Something different, something intangible. His speed was good, he was now climbing up into the village. The air feels cool against his face. It was a wonderful day.

Worlds collide and merge. Time separates. A driver pulls up. A motorbike lies on the side of the road, it is a twisted carcass. The rider has been thrown against a tree. He is dead, his neck is broken and his face is twisted in agony and pain. Across the road a cyclist lies beside his bike. The cyclist lies still, with a slight smile across his face, he is unconscious.

Annie had watched him through the night. Jake was still unconscious, it had been three days. The doctors were feeding him by a tube. Oxygen being given to help him breathe. Jake had no broken bones, just bruises. Without his helmet he would have been dead. There was a swelling and a bleed in the brain. The doctors were hopeful, they had tried to bring him around. So far, Jake had not responded.

During the night she'd noticed a twitch, the slightest of movements, around the eyes. It happened again forty minutes later.

"Jake, Jake can you hear me?"

There was no response. She called a nurse, who had suggested Annie get some sleep. The nurse had checked the monitor on the wall. The heart rate was steady, maybe a little high, the oxygen was good. Jake's blood pressure could have been from a man half his age.

Annie sat back in her chair, watching. Jake, unshaven, looked peaceful with the slightest of smiles on his face. The window was black with the night's darkness and a reflection of the light in the room.

In the hospital corridor, outside Jake's room, staff

were arriving and taking their coats off, a trolley was being pushed around. The day was waking. Annie awoke to a hand on her shoulder and a gentle voice.

"Go lie down and get some proper sleep." Remembering the twitches in the night Annie replied.

"I'll just wait for the doctor."

The routines of the ward take over. Another nurse came in, looked at the figures on the screen, and made some notes. Eventually two doctors entered. Annie explained about the twitch and the movement.

"Just a spasm," the first doctor replied.

"It happens quite a lot."

Even so, the doctors looked through the night's readings, they scroll back on the screen. Yes, there was something. Every forty minutes, or so, the heart rate increased, the breathing deepened. The doctors seem puzzled and looked again at the numbers and wavy lines.

As the doctors leave, Annie noticed the little

twitch again, around Jake's eyes. She moved her chair a little closer, knocking the stand with the tubes and the feeding machine. She pictured the day when Jake was leaning over her in hospital when they had their first boy, and squeezes Jake's hand.

It's a glorious day. Jake is going faster than ever. Soon it will be the descent, the little bend, the ride into the village. There it is, the Déjà vu, he feels it, this has happened before. Jake pictures his wife in hospital with their first child, he hears her shouting, he feels her hand in his. There is a sound in the wind, he thinks he hears someone calling him. 'Jake.' Looking over the fence he sees and hears a sheep bleating. He leans forward again. It was a wonderful ride.

A doctor came in, and placed his hand on Annie's shoulder. Annie is holding Jake's hand and softly calling his name. The doctor's voice is calm and warm. "Don't worry, he'll wake up soon."

The Right Sort

Bernie swung into the Ivy's car park. The restaurant had been getting great reviews. The wide tyres of his Aston Martin crackled across the gravel as he parked close to the entrance. Then, sitting back in the rich leather seat, Bernie looked through the window. Pristine tables, dressed in white, waited for the coming night. Empty crystal glasses sparkled in the sunlight. Vivian would like this!

The place held fond memories for both of them. The last time they were here, he was riding a real leather Brookes saddle. Now, that was real old-school cycling.

Back then it had been a busy eggs and chips café. The riders from the Velo and Wheelers all stopped here, just before the big climbs out in the Peaks. When was that? The railings they parked their bikes against were still there. But now freshly painted. He could picture Viv seated on a bench, surrounded by riders scrabbling for toast and tea. Fuel, food and drink, to get them over the hills. Bernie's favourite was beans on hot buttered crumpets. He could see them on the plate, mmmm, tasty.

Vivian had always caught the eyes of the men in the club. Of course. Viv was gorgeous. But it was far more, the deep blue eyes, her smile. Bernie smiled as he thought of the café and Vivian. This really was a great idea.

Inside, Jack and Stella were going over the figures. They'd sunk everything into the Ivy, all their savings and a second mortgage. It had been their dream for years. The restaurant had received good reviews. Business had been steady, even growing. But it wasn't enough. They could see through the figures to a bleak future.

What more could they do? They'd made something of the old place and worked hard. It had been an old café, unused for years with lino floors and dirty benches.

The previous owner had died intestate. It had taken years to sort it out before the café could be finally sold. Now it looked wonderful, elegant, marvellous. Somewhere special. Even so, the numbers didn't stack up. They'd pared the business down to the bones and it wasn't making any money.

Still, they still had a few months. It could work. People were coming, they just weren't spending enough. They simply needed more of the right sort of customers.

Stella looked up, hearing the tyres on the gravel. Seeing the gleaming golden Aston Martin, she called back to Jack.

"We need this!"

They both stood up and went to the door to greet Bernie. They really did need the business. Bernie was looking for a venue for a large dinner party.

It was Viv's last ride in the series for the ladies handicap trophy: the club hundred mile time trial. Bernie was following behind in his Rolls Royce. It was embarrassing, but Viv needed Bernie's support. She kept the pace as high as she could, her legs were beginning to ache, the road was getting rough. She was flagging.

Viv had been trying for the trophy for years and never quite managed it. This year she was ahead of the others by quite a few points. Even so, she needed to get a good time.

Vivian pushed hard on the pedals, keeping an

even tempo. She could see Bernie, if she looked back, wearing that blasted flat cap. His head peering over the steering wheel. She'd have something to say about that! She knew Bernie was planning something. Bernie was always planning and trying to surprise her. Even after all these years.

"Shit!" Viv shouted at the road. The front tyre had blown out on a pot hole, she hadn't been concentrating and was tired.

The cycling fall−off faeries had been calling her. The sirens of the road. She rolled to a stop. Bernie was immediately out of the car and had taken a spare wheel off the back seat.

"No problem Viv, don't panic, just a few seconds."

Bernie was relaxed and calm. Reaching down, he soon had the wheel out of the forks. A few turns on the quick release and the new wheel was back in and tightened. Viv was ready to get going again.

"C'mon Viv, you can do it!"

Viv pushed on again and was soon up to speed. Bernie was a little further back in the Rolls. Between the two of them, they were the King and Queen of the roads.

It was beginning to rain. Funnily, Bernie knew that would help. When things got worse they both worked even harder. It was in their nature. They still rode together, but mostly on the plains. Bernie's knees weren't so good and it had been a few years since they had ridden over the hills. Now the Peaks were a day trip out in the car and some gentle hiking in the hills.

Up ahead, Mac was at the side of the road. Bernie slowed down as he passed. He pressed a button, the window slid down.

"Mac, are you okay?" The rain felt cool.

"I'm packing! Just blown a tyre and it's cold out here."

"Need a lift?" Mac looked tired, he hadn't

done well in these time trials for years. They were both fighting the years. It was warm in the Rolls.

"I've phoned my son, he'll be here in a few minutes, get going and keep an eye on Viv!"

All those years ago they'd both been hoping to woo Viv. Viv still had a soft spot for Mac and sometimes persuaded Bernie to give him a hand. Last time, by selling him one of the company's old vans at a knocked down price.

"Mac, how's that van I sold you?"

Mac looked into the Rolls at Bernie. Somewhere back in time he'd just missed with Vivian. He knew Viv had persuaded Bernie to sell him the van.

"Great, but get going, Viv's getting on."

Viv was the bond between the two. Mac was right, Bernie needed to get up to her in case she had another problem.

Soon he was back behind Viv, the rain had

picked up. It wasn't a good day to ride. Bernie leaned over and opened the glove box. In it was a vacuum flask. He gingerly opened it, and poured out a cup of hot sweet coffee. Just how Viv liked it.

Driving up beside her he opened the window and passed the coffee to her. Viv took the cup and took a few gulps spilling a little on the black top for the gods of the road.

"Thanks." Bernie was a soft old fool at times, he'd do everything he could for her. She really did love him.

"Not so far now, keep it going." Bernie encouraged her on and took the cup back. He glanced down at the odometer. Just under fifteen miles to go. Viv was hurting, it would seem much further to her. Bernie said nothing more and dropped back. He could do no more, it was now up to Viv.

Bernie had always been a cyclist, but his money had come from haulage and hard work. He'd been lucky. Bernie could remember his first contract like it was yesterday, he'd had to rent the truck.

Combining driving with cycling had been hard, he'd often put a bike in the back of the cabin and fit a time trial into the journey. It meant some uncomfortable nights, sleeping in the cabin with the bike. Waking early and riding a fifty or hundred and then finishing the job. Mostly it was shifting aggregates. Gravel from the local quarries.

Over a good few years he'd built up a big business re—investing in trucks. And with Viv's help he'd found some good drivers. Those early years were hard. Viv had always been good been with money and managed the company's finances. Her mother, a Yorkshire woman, had married a Frenchman, a cyclist. It was a fiery combination. Cycling and saving money were in Viv's blood.

Usually, ideas came to him when he was cycling. But he'd been following Viv for a few hours now and was getting hungry. That's when it came to him. A big dinner! It will have to be somewhere good. He remembered a review of the Ivy.

Viv was soaking. She'd just passed the line and pulled over. Bernie overtook and parked the Rolls in the lay by just up ahead. He passed Viv a towel and starting putting the bike in the back of the Rolls.

"You did it!" Bernie beamed with a big smile.

"You're finally going to get the trophy."

Viv didn't look that happy, but managed to return a faint smile.

"C'mon, let's get you warmed up." Bernie put his arm around her and guided her to the Rolls. Inside it was warm, the old leather seat cradled her. Bernie had been rolling around in comfort and luxury while she had been on that blasted bike. Viv couldn't help herself.

"Why don't you get a proper car, this is an old man's car, you can afford something better!"

Bernie felt a little hurt, but didn't let it show. He'd always wanted a Rolls Royce. And as soon as he could afford one, he'd bought it. Even before the house. Maybe he should change it? It had been his pride and joy for years. Mostly it stayed in the garage, as he cycled when he wasn't working. But when he was driving the Rolls he felt like the king of the road. Still, maybe it was time for a change.

Viv had mentioned the Aston Martin when they had watched a Bond movie. It seemed a good choice and would be another great surprise for Viv.

However, it almost hadn't happened. Shortly after Viv's trophy—winning time trial, Bernie had visited the dealer. On getting out of the Rolls he'd been warmly greeted by the salesman. Bernie had soon agreed to buy the Aston Martin.

"One last thing!" Bernie had remembered just in time. "I need to check I can get my bike in the back!"

The salesman had laughed, thinking Bernie was joking. The laughing quickly subsided as Bernie headed over to the Rolls, opened the boot, and then headed back to the Aston Martin with a bike in his arms.

Somewhat aghast, the salesman reluctantly opened the Aston Martin's boot. Before he could even think about covering the floor, Bernie was wrestling the bike into the back. It was clearly a squeeze and hadn't been designed to take a bike. But Bernie soon had the front wheel off and the bike fitted in. Only now there was a streak of grease on the leather mat in the boot. Bernie turned around and held his hand out to the salesman.

"Sold." Bernie was happy, very happy, it would be a great surprise for Viv. Best of all Viv loved it!

Back at the Ivy, Bernie was planning the next surprise and explained to Jack and Stella the details of the party for his wife, he needed a venue for about seventy five guests. Could they do it?

Stella looked at Jack. This one evening would solve their financial worries; for a while. Bernie had seemed more than happy with the price. Luckily Jack had made the connection. He'd seen Bernie's surname on the card and asked if he was anything to do with the haulage company.

"I sold the company a few years ago and retired." Bernie smiled. "It was a good job"

Jack and Stella walked Bernie through the menu, explaining how only the finest local ingredients were used. Bernie had asked about the mussels.

"They're from Scotland!" Stella explained.

"And for vegetarians?" Bernie asked.

"We can have a special menu!" This time Jack had been quick to answer. The only vegetarian dish was lasagne and it wasn't great. "Our chef is renowned."

Bernie couldn't help seeing himself sitting at a

bench in the old café after riding in the rain and filling up on baked beans on hot buttered crumpets.

Bernie sat down in a chair where one of the benches would have been. Viv was going to love this, it was a good idea and would be another great surprise. Viv deserved it.

"Pudding, sweet?" Bernie queried.

Jack like a flash passed over the sweet menu. The list was a literary feast of bonbons, bombes, coulis and sorbets.

Again Bernie couldn't help think about the flapjack that Pete used to serve at the café. Pete, the owners name came to him, a ghost of a memory, Bernie wondered what had happened to him?

Jack and Stella sat down with Bernie for over an hour. They ironed out all of the details for Viv's special night. Stella talked and was full of ideas while Jack made notes. They needed to get this right.

Bernie was just the sort of customer they were

hoping to get. Bernie had soon made his decision and after wrapping things up started to make his way out. He held out his hand to Jack, and after saying his goodbyes, turned to face the door.

The golden Aston Martin was smiling at him through the door. Bernie reached down for the handle and caught sight of the sign. Turning back to Jack and Stella one last time, and with a slightly cooler voice, said he'd be in touch.

Even after all these years Bernie couldn't quite believe it. Getting back in the car and turning on the engine with the push of a button. He muttered to himself. I guess the party will have to be at the Waltzing Weasel. Yes, Viv would still like that!

Jack and Stella were pleased, they watched Bernie drive out of the car park in his Aston Martin. It looked like their financial worries would soon be over. Things were beginning to look up.

As they started to tidy up after Bernie's visit,

Stella could hear some more wheels and voices coming into the car park. She looked up and walked over to the door. The people looked tired and grubby from the road. The riders walked uncomfortably on the gravel as they wheeled their bikes to the railing and locked them up. They then headed back over to the Ivy's door. Stella frowned, and with a slightly raised and annoyed voice, shouted to Jack.

"They keep turning up!"

Stella checked the door was locked and bolted, and after turning the sign outwards for the riders to see, headed into the kitchen.

Jerry, from the Wheelers, looked down at the sign. In big bold letters it simply said: 'No Cyclists!'

Rewards

Joe's thighs ached. Yet he was thundering along fast. Really fast. Gravel was spitting away from his tyres. How was he doing it? His bike's wheels were whistling and sighing. Where was it coming from? Joe forced himself forward, leaning low, cutting through the morning air. Maybe it was the new *tubs.* Tubular tyres cemented onto the rim, with the inner tube sewn in.

Only two weeks earlier, on an evening run, Andy had sailed past him. Joe had been training hard and a long ride, three days earlier, had taken its toll on his legs. They were empty. It was no excuse, Joe abandoned and went home deflated. Sometimes you had to listen to the legs.

In the mirror was an apparition; was it then or now? Joe looked down. On the doormat was the invitation he'd been expecting. He struggled to bend down and pick up the envelope. Straightening up, he caught the image of himself, a reflection. Was it really him? He was tall and strong, cycle shorts stretched over immense thighs. Shoulders were big and wide, hair dark and full. A woollen cycling jersey, a little worn, covered his broad chest. Eyes, bright blue, were sharp and alive.

The apparition faded. Joe's eyes were still blue, but now his complexion was ruddy and his hair grey. He looked down at his ever widening girth, he'd stopped looking at the scales years ago. Joe still rode a bike, but now for only a few miles. The years, and steroids for arthritis, painted an unforgiving picture on his body. He accepted it. There was no choice.

Despite his girth, Joe was still a member of the Wheelers. The club was a big part of his life. For years, even after the accident, he'd been the club chairman. As a rider he'd been a specialist in the time trial holding the club fifty record for thirty–three years.

That was a long time ago. In the mirror it had been today, that day, the day Joe would crush the record. The day when he would dig deep and give everything to the road.

Just up ahead was the blue Jersey. He'd close him down before the roundabout and the return to the start. It was the first lap, how had he managed to catch him so quickly? He passed the rider; not even a look. Sweat dripped off Joe's cap. The bike flew over a rough section just before the roundabout. Joe looked up.

Everything was good, the course marshals waved him on, shouting:

"Clear!"

Joe wasn't going to mess it up. Leaning the bike into the turn, he kept pedalling. Passing the blue jersey again, now on the other side of the road, he headed back to the start line. Did he feel a wind behind him? He raised his weight above the seat and cranks, just the slightest of movements, to put even more force on the pedals. Now to keep it smooth. Andy was up ahead.

It was early morning, very early. Since 1932, even during the war, the club's open fifty was held on the first Sunday in June. Joe signed on and changed at the roadside. There were no changing rooms, just a screen held up by friends. If you were lucky.

It was a good day to ride, there was the lightest of breezes and a cool morning air. The roads were empty, race marshals stood on the course corners. Spectators, mostly riders' families, gathered at the start line.

Joe had come fourth in the draw for starting position. Andy, having drawn second, would set off two minutes earlier.

They both had arrived early so they could warm up before the race. Joe felt a little sick and Andy had been chatting nervously but was now quiet. They were both lost to their inner landscape. Preparing.

The race, an open event, was part of a national series. Riders from other clubs could compete. At the start many were still preparing with help from supporters. Numbers were being pinned on jerseys and water bottles filled.

In his working life, Joe was a toolmaker, a craftsman. Decades had passed since he served his apprenticeship. It was different now, tools and instruments were made by machines and computers. Joe used his hands, a keen eye, experience and skill. Guided by a drawing, he would turn metal stock into fine tools and instruments.

Joe still worked when he was needed. There were the 'Specials'. Those jobs requiring his fine skills, a craftsman's eye and hand finishing. It was an art, completing the Specials, they were made from expensive and exotic materials like platinum and gold. Moulding, casting and precision machining were all needed. There were only a few craftsman left that could do the job, especially with his background. Jobs were becoming rarer, orders were thin on the ground.

Joe suspected he was taking too long. He liked to get it right and that took care and time. It had taken him two attempts to get the last job right.

When finally finished, he'd sign the job with two tiny initials on the side of the piece, and then find a nice case. A case that was simple and not overstated, something functional. He imagined the customer opening the case for the final reveal, and inspecting his work. Joe pictured them checking the job met their specifications; that it would last and be fit for purpose.

The start came quickly. You were never really ready. Joe watched Andy setting off, while waiting in line. In another minute the next rider followed, Joe's minute man. An outsider from a distant club, young and strong and wearing a blue jersey. Andy had looked good and set off smoothly. Joe's feet were strapped into the pedals, he was being held by the pusher−off. The time keeper was counting down.

A time trial record stands against all pretenders. The record is a culmination of skill, inspiration, effort and luck. All converge as a stopwatch marks moments of utter exhaustion. A rider can be defeated by anything and everything. The conspiracy of obstacles to a record is endless. Weather, traffic, road surface, the bike. A gust of wind, a vehicle in the way, gravel across the road, a soft tyre, injury. A multitude of minutiae protect a record from any assault.

Joe looked down and tapped his thighs and frowned, thinking 'they'd better be ready.'

The pusher−off held him steady. The time keeper tapped Joe's shoulder.

"Ready!"

"Three." Joe breathed easily.

"Two." The countdown continued.

Joe felt the tension in his legs and the pusher−off supporting him. He steadied himself.

"One. Go."

Joe kicked, only to find that one of the straps was loose and his foot slipped. Shit. He almost fell as he leaned down, pushing his foot back in, pulling at the strap. The pusher−off just managed to keep him from falling, but time was lost. Joe was angry at himself. It was a rookie mistake.

Up ahead, the blue jersey; now way−off in the distance. Joe kept his head low and started to work the pedals. He'd nothing to lose and started pushing his legs hard. There was work to do. His lungs, giant bellows, fired up the furnace of his muscles with oxygen. The start, soon a distant memory, had been a disaster, but a fifty was about balance and pacing. He could still do a good time. Focus is drawn into the few metres ahead. Joe looked up, he could see a flash of blue.

This course was simple, out and back, two laps. Twenty-five miles each lap. A course where you could see the earlier riders returning on the other side of the road. You then had a measure of how well you were doing or not.

It was the second lap, Andy was on the other side of the road, grimacing and looking white, heading back to the finish line. Joe made the final turn at the roundabout and was following fast.

Again the marshals shouted:

"Clear."

Andy was up the road. Joe put his head down, gripped the bars and pushed. He'd managed to get a few mouthfuls of water. His mouth was dry and lungs rasping.

There must be a wind behind him. He looked at

the grass and trees for clues. Rattling the chain he pushed the cranks. He was closing in. Joe had passed the blue jersey and another rider who'd started ahead of him on the first lap. Only Andy was in front. He looked behind. He knew he shouldn't have, the road behind was empty. There were, however, a few riders on the other side of the road heading for the roundabout. They stared at Joe.

Joe caught Andy just before the final stretch to the finish and could see Andy's face, he looked terrible.

"Go on Joe." Andy had cracked but urged Joe on. "Keep going, you can do it!"

Joe had been invited to be the guest speaker and present the trophy for the annual club fifty. The record, his record, had finally fallen. There wasn't a trophy in Joe's day. He had the cutting from the magazine, Cycling Weekly, in a scrapbook. Joe's name, position and time were printed with the results of the other races around the country. It was a long list and there were many clubs and many races.

A month after taking the record, Joe was in a bad accident. Just after leaving Andy, after another evening run, a car had come out from a side road and struck him in the side, fracturing his leg in several places.

The recovery had been long. Very long. Weeks had turned to months and then years before Joe was riding again. Of course he rode again and committed as much to the club as ever. Year after year he worked as a course marshal, or pusher−off and sometimes even timekeeper.

In a fifty, there's time to think. As the legs burn the fuel and the tank is emptied, the body starts sending the simplest of messages to the brain. 'Stop! What the hell are you doing?' And 'Where's the fire?'

The brain then starts recalling anything that may help. Pedal in circles. Count in threes. Imagine a string pulling up at the knees. Think of scraping the snow off your shoe at the bottom of the stroke. Sit back, keep going! Breathe easily, deeply, regularly. Every coach had something different to say.

Joe gripped the bars, held his position and kept his position low. He was lost in the rhythm of the bike and the sound of the road. He knew he was moving fast, but could he keep it going?

As for Joe's skills in toolmaking, he used these in repairing and maintaining the club's bikes, especially the difficult repairs. If a repair was possible then Joe could do it, even when all others had failed.

The annual dinner was held in the function room at the Waltzing Weasel, the home of the Wheelers. Photographs around the room echoed the long history of the club. Former riders looked out from the past. In one corner stood Joe, in black and white, he had just finished his record ride. The image faded, but, still, the ride could be seen in the sweat and dirt on Joe's face.

"You can do it!"

Joe had heard Andy's words. There were still ten miles to go. His legs burning, his throat dry, his arms shaking. But he could do it. He was doing it. The effort was lost to the road. The sweat was dripping into his eyes, they were bloodshot and sore.

The finish. Where had the last ten miles gone? Joe was exhausted, there was no more to give. Seeing him teetering, two spectators stepped out and stopped him falling. They helped him off the bike and unstrapped his feet. Joe collapsed to the floor. After a short while he stood up and brushed himself down. A camera flashed. Someone had taken a photograph. Joe had broken the course record.

Like a rider's strength during a long time trial, there had been a rise and fall in the Wheelers membership. A new wave of riders filled the seats at the annual club meeting that for many years had been empty. Now there was a new excitement and enthusiasm. Cycling was booming again. New talents were taking up the challenges and Joe's record had finally been broken.

Joe called Chris, the new record holder, up to accept the trophy. Chris and Joe had talked earlier, congratulating each other. The two riders, separated by generations, greeted each other like old friends, with hands outstretched. Joe had a big smile on his face. Having recalled the tale of his ride, he was more than happy to pass the record and trophy on to Chris.

Both riders knew the effort, the love of cycling that had enabled them to push their bodies to the limit, to compete. As their eyes met they both felt that spirit of competition, of not losing, of fighting to the edge. And they both gave a nod of deep respect. Chris looked much like Joe's apparition in the hallway mirror. Young and strong, with dark hair, strong shoulders and a broad chest. Joe tapped his mid-section and made a small joke.

The new trophy was bright silver and very grand. As the record holder Chris could hold it for a year and then return it to the club. Chris's name was engraved on a plaque at the base.

The club chairman sitting at the high table rattled a spoon against a glass, bringing the room to an unexpected stillness.

The room was mostly quiet, a few whispers could be heard around the room. Joe looked back to the chairman who, now standing, asked and waved Joe and Chris to take to their seats.

"Everyone here knows the story of Joe's, and Chris's record!"

"It has taken thirty–three years for Chris to come along and better Joe's time!"

There were a few raised voices and a few claps. The Chairman quietened the room.

"And finally we have a new record."

This time the chairman encouraged a big wave

of applause for Chris and then waited for it to subside.

"However, as well as celebrating Chris's great achievement we are also here to recognise Joe's commitment and years of service to the club."

Another wave of applause arose from around the room. The chairman turned to Joe, who was now bright red in the face and looking genuinely shocked and surprised.

"Today, we would like to give Joe an award for his long service to the club."

"We all know there wasn't a trophy when Joe last broke the record, but we hope that this award will give him great pleasure and be a permanent reminder of how he's thought of, by everyone in the club."

The Chairman gestured to Joe.

"C'mon up Joe. This is for you!"

Joe stood up to accept the award. The chairman held out his hand, in it was a box. A red case.

Joe looked down with recognition. The case was

simple, functional, not overstated. Joe took the case lightly into his hands. He'd always imagined the customer inspecting his work. With the deepest of smiles, and knowledge of what lay within, Joe opened the case.

Taking out the medal, the 'Special' he'd worked on for over a month, Joe looked at it with new eyes. It was a work of art, a work of precision, passion, and love. He held the piece, the medal, his own work. His two tiny initials were on the side and now his name had been engraved on the back. The medal felt warm to touch and at home in his hands. Joe looked up with tears in his eyes, finally lost for words.

The club members clearly hadn't known Joe had made the award in his hands. But the medal, his medal made from platinum and gold, was a symbol of everything that Joe had given, and loved and made in his life. This truly was a wonderful night.

Motivation

I would like to give you a kick up the royal arse. But that won't work. Some say the trick is to give yourself a set of rules. But I feel the only thing that will work is if you are 'motivated'. And your simple comments suggest that you may not be. Eating and activity are culturally dominated. You are told that you are 'ageing'. You are told your body will not stay 'young'. You are told you will not be 'motivated'. You are sold 'food', you eat even when you are not hungry. You look less at the women and you no longer expect them to look at you. You imagine that you are old. You have a frame of reference that includes 'young' people. Your partner teases you about your looks and weight. Maybe a reflection. You accept the light hearted humour and jest. It's who you are, isn't it? This is your life.

This year on one sunny day, I went cycling in Mallorca with Gerry. We went out for a long ride over the Mallorca mountains. On our first testing climb, despite taking it gently before, Gerry charged ahead, determined to get away from me. I quietly increased my effort and sat behind him, surprised by his change in tempo just because it was a climb. At the top he then sat back and we cycled to the beginning of the Mountain range north of the Island: the Lluc Monastery climb from Selva. The start of the day's heavy duty climbing. On the way, Gerry took it easy and we chatted.

Then we arrived at the base of the Lluc climb at

Selva; a climb cyclists train on for the Tour. Off Gerry went. Again. Picking up my pace, I was getting close to the limit. All the time Gerry was about twenty-five metres in front. I measured my effort and kept him at that distance. Too close and Gerry would make even more effort. The trick was to sit at a distance where he couldn't hear me, and just cycle steadily.

We climbed the bends, they kept coming. The climb is almost a thousand metres. But cyclists know there is a café stop at the top, a rest, coffee and cake, pizza and water. Gerry kept going and I followed. We were passing everyone on the mountain. Sometimes they looked like they were standing still. I was quite amazed. This was the fastest long climb I'd ever done.

Some riders, sensing the effort, gave us a nod and a cheer. We quietly kept going, pushing steadily, each with our own thoughts. Our own motivation.

We had a few more bends to go. Gerry was tiring now. Feeling his effort, I moved closer but had to drop back so he didn't charge off again. I was sure if he heard me, even if tired, he would try harder.

Knowing the climb and that the café was just round another corner I slowly picked up my pace. Gerry was still tiring, his head was down now. I found myself making a little effort, I couldn't resist and rolled into the café alongside him and patted him on the back. It was the best long climb I'd ever done. I was amazed at my fitness and control. On the edge, but with judgement. But Gerry had driven us both up the mountain. No one passed. We were kings for those few moments.

As we slowly recovered in the Café, I could see that Gerry had made a big effort, it was like he had ridden the climb of his life. He explained that he had not quite judged it right and forgotten the last two switchbacks. He ate like a horse and drank loads, preparing for the coming climbs. We had more to do!

I remember almost every mile of that day. Where

we fixed his puncture. Where we took our photographs. Where we had our lunch. It was wonderful. Sadly my cycling computer ran out of batteries and I lost the ride so it is not recorded. But the bends, the roads, and Gerry's company made it a special day. The next climb was the Puig Major.

Gerry had calf muscles the size of my thighs and maybe that's where his story started. It will not motivate you and cannot. But he made me proud of what we had both done that day. Me, near fifty, and Gerry, who three years earlier had major heart surgery.

Gerry carried the scar. The zip, where they split the sternum to gain access to the heart. You wouldn't know unless he decided to show you. Each morning before work, he would go cycling for four hours. Gerry explained how he started cycling and how he had physically changed. He talked about the strong winds where he lived and about how far it was to the nearest hill. What really motivated Gerry? I still don't know and definitely couldn't explain.

My motivation? I had trained and worked hard. I was ready for that climb and the following ones to come. I understood my body. The limits, the emotions that would rise and fall. The calling of the body to the mind to stop. The depth of breath required. The control to sit at the edge of physical effort and no further. An understanding of what the human body can really do. And utterly, the desire not to be beaten. Not to win, but not to give up. To hold on, to take the challenge, to grip it, squeeze it. To focus and to remember that I am who I am and not what anybody else tells me.

I am not an age or a concept. I am simply me and I absolutely love killing these mountains. I hope you find your motivation. Because it would be a truly great experience to share the roads with you and I like to imagine you there with me.

That ride with Gerry was the ride of a lifetime,

but the mountains are always waiting for us. Of course, these challenges are just a game, a twinkle, and at heart I'm just a little boy escaping school. A little anxious, a little guilty, but what a thrill.

The Hotel Son Llàtzer

Cyclists are often drawn to the Son Llàtzer in Mallorca. Those that know it, will know it well. If you are lucky, your room will have a picture window overlooking the plains. With the high mountains on the left and the monastery of Cura peeking up on the right.

The reception is efficient, the staff will quickly take your details and soon show you to your room. You may have to wait a short while. Your thoughts, no doubt, will be on the bike and the road. Riding the roads of Mallorca is both a pleasure and an addiction. For many it's a way of life. Each year, thousands embark on the spring migration. Training camps are full. Roads are alive, *peletons* drive speeds up, as groups of riders fight the early spring winds. Old friends meet up again. A year or two may have passed since they last met. New friendships are made. Routes are discussed, café stops are planned, cycling stories are told. Everyone is keen to get going.

Meanwhile at the Son Llàtzer, the staff are busy, food is prepared, rooms are cleaned, beds are made, and floors are swept. There is a lot of work to do for the guests. Every meal is carefully planned. Sometimes basic, but everything needed for a cyclist to recover from the road. The staff, like angels, will do their very best to make you comfortable. To wake up in the Son Llàtzer is to hear a soft voice announcing the day.

"Buenos Dias". Often it is almost whispered.

Having planned and trained, Kenny had looked

forward to getting to Mallorca. He'd brought his best bike. It was soon unpacked, checked and assembled. Made from carbon fibre, and using the latest Campagnolo super record group set, it was a great bike.

Sometimes you share a room at the Son Llàtzer, this was one of those occasions. Kenny's companion was Pedro, whose family was originally from Mallorca. Pedro had been having difficulty sleeping and the two had chatted into the night.

Kenny lay on the bed next to Pedro, recovering from the road. It had been a hard, very hard day. Everything ached. The conversations meandered lazily between Pedro and himself, always coming back to bikes. This time it had moved on to religion. For Kenny, cycling was as close to religion as he ever wanted.

"What religion are the men in suits from?" Pedro enquired.

"What men in suits?" Kenny wasn't quite sure what Pedro was talking about.

"Here in Mallorca, they come from England, and knock on the door."

Kenny couldn't quite believe his ears. It was easy to guess. It was bad enough they knocked on his own door back in Yorkshire. But to hear that they were here in Mallorca! Kenny uttered a few choice Yorkshire words under his breath. He held back, Pedro wouldn't understand them. He spoke, leaning towards Pedro.

"Jehovah's Witnesses, I guess."

"What religion are they?" Pedro looked puzzled.

"Christians." Kenny carried on.

"I thought the Mallorcan people were very religious?" Kenny remembered cycling through a big parade in a village one Easter. He'd felt like an interloper from another planet. Palm leaves were scattered on the road. A colourful procession announced and celebrated their beliefs.

"It used to be so." Pedro replied, and then carried on. "At one time, in my village at Muro, there were ten priests. Ten! Now there is only one."

Kenny was genuinely surprised. He couldn't help himself think about the immigrants in his own town. The old library had recently been converted into a mosque.

It was funny to imagine Jehovah's Witnesses from Yorkshire, knocking on a bemused Spanish family's door.

"Ay up!" Kenny could picture the Jehovah's Witnesses waving a leaflet, with a cheery smile, as the door was closed on them yet again.

"They knock on my door!" Kenny motioned "And I wave them away!"

They both laughed, Pedro was yawning, it looked like he'd had a hard day as well.

As Kenny lay back on the bed he considered the day. The ride had gone well. Mostly. The first ride of the holiday, it was hard to believe. The roads were like old friends, they usually treated him well. There had been some good efforts today, not too hard. With a couple of weeks of training he'd wanted to build up slowly. Kenny smiled to himself at the thought of building up slowly, as he really felt the, more than usual, aches of the day.

Meanwhile, when Kenny had been out riding in the morning, the Son Llàtzer had buzzed with guests coming and going. Some staying for just a night, while others would be staying for a few weeks. Taxis came and went, and the bus stop just outside the main entrance was busy. At the reception a sign announced that free wifi was available. A few people peered into their phones. Several sat with laptops at the reception. The Son Llàtzer had all the latest technologies to make a visit comfortable. Kenny's own visit had started with

178

a ride in the hotel's minivan.

He remembered the relief when they had picked him and his bike up. Kenny had memories of Doug, the trip organiser, telling him that the Son Llàtzer was one of the best places in Mallorca. Apparently he'd spent a whole month there, one spring.

For a first day, the morning's ride had gone well. Kenny had taken it easy, there would be plenty of time in the coming weeks for some real tests. Today's ride was about getting used to long rides and the rhythm of the day−on−day riding.

Riding, resting and sleeping. Lazy evenings just having a long meal followed by relaxing in the local café. It was a routine Kenny loved, it was a retreat from the worries of everyday life back at home. No job, no phone. Just riding and recovery. He'd been looking forward to it for months.

That morning, Kenny had chased down some

riders along the coast road after he'd warmed up. There had been a strong head wind. Once he'd caught up with the small group he sat on the wheel of the last rider gathering his strength. After a few minutes, he'd kicked out again and started to pull away. He felt strong, it was going to be a good couple of weeks.

Rides have texture. They change, going from bad to good as a rider recovers in the saddle. Or, from good to bad. The mind plays tricks, the body doesn't respond. The road kicks back.

Light clouds had been building up and scudding across the sky, they were getting darker. The last thing Kenny wanted, was to be caught out in the rain.

Storms come in quickly on the island. Kenny remembered one spring, sheltering by a rock wall for half an hour, crouching together with a couple of other riders. They had been pelted by ice during a massive storm. The dry road had become a torrent.

Only a few minutes earlier, it had been a balmy twenty five degrees. It wasn't a good memory. The storm had lasted longer than expected and they eventually had to start riding to get to some cover.

The water had been up to the axles on the wheels. As the group had finally made it into town, a bolt of lightning had cracked down just a few meters from them. Eventually they made their way to a café to wait out the storm. They'd sat like drowned rats, warming up. A waitress had kindly given them a couple of blankets.

The storm had been bad. That day Palma airport had to be closed for two hours and it made the news. Videos could be found on YouTube showing flooded towns. It was a good story for the café, but they could've done without it.

Today, Kenny had cycled through into the afternoon and made a short stop for some fuel: a sports drink and some sweets. The stop went to plan, he parked the bike in the usual spot. Thoughts of the route back filled his mind as he planned his efforts. Easy for a while, and then hard back to the coast, and fast in the last twenty kilometres. A few drops of rain spotted the road, it was time to get going again. With a steady pace, Kenny started the ride back. The air was warm, the few drops of rain had soon stopped.

Adrenalin. Shock. The bike slides away. How? Water, maybe oil, a thin film. A car brakes. Questions!

"Are you okay?" A young man leant over Kenny.

"Can I help?"

Gentle movement. Pain. Then no pain. Only adrenalin. Thoughts multiply. Emotions. Then immediately a deep knowledge. The shoulder. The collarbone was broken, maybe more. The brain was working at high speed, processing what to do, what could be done. Get to the side of the road. How's the bike?

"Are you okay?" The voice came again.

"Can I help?" A young man helped Kenny get to his feet.

Kenny formulated a plan, almost unconsciously. 'Get back to the hotel. Get to the Son Llàtzer,' he stood there, muttering to himself.

"I'm okay, I'll be all right." Kenny picked up the bike and moved to the side of the road. The young man followed looking anxious.

"Are you sure? There's a clinic nearby!" After a short while the young man, satisfied that the fallen rider was okay, got back in his car and drove on.

Kenny was now alone, he'd tried to get back on his bike. It was too bad. He'd have to call the hotel. They'd come and pick him up. He could wait. Kenny watched two riders going around the same roundabout at the same speed. They didn't fall. The rain was pouring down. Only minutes before, there had been blue skies and light clouds. After fumbling in his pockets to find his phone, he rang the hotel.

"I'm going to need a lift, I've broken my shoulder." Kenny winced, but stayed calm.

The hotel sent a van. Dimly, Kenny remembered the crack of his helmet as he hit the deck. He waited. Another car stopped, the driver leaned out and asked if he needed help. Kenny explained that someone was coming to pick him up. He wasn't sure they understood. The driver wound up the window against the rain and drove on.

Two Dutch riders passed by. Kenny flagged them down and asked if they would stay with him until he was picked up. He'd realised he may pass out. The pain was creeping in. Kenny's face was pale. The Dutch riders waited with him and asked about the fall.

"The bike fell away, maybe oil or dampness?" Kenny had seen nothing on the road.

The deeper knowledge ran through Kenny's thoughts. The hospital, the weeks ahead. The slow recovery. Sleepless nights. His first day, his first ride. Kenny felt cheated.

The hotel's minivan arrived. The bike was soon safely loaded in the back. Kenny struggled to get in after thanking the two Dutch riders. They were soon glad to be back on their way, the rain was lashing down

Boris, the hotel manager, had driven out to fetch Kenny and asked if he wanted to go back to the hotel.

"No, I've broken my collarbone. Straight to the Son Llàtzer!" Kenny winced with pain.

As many cyclists know, the Son Llàtzer is not a hotel. Like it's namesake Lazarus, it has a second life. It is, in fact, the finest modern hospital in Mallorca. Boris drove quickly through the storm, he could feel Kenny's disappointment. They were both quiet on the journey. Kenny managed the pain while Boris concentrated on driving through the storm. The wipers were working hard to clear the rain from the windscreen.

On arrival at the Son Llàtzer, Kenny's details were quickly taken, and after the shortest of waits he was taken to the x—ray department. The diagnosis was of a broken collarbone, scapular and two fractured ribs. It had been a hard fall. Kenny was sent to a larger x—ray scanner to check his lungs hadn't been damaged by his fractured ribs. They were clear.

Afterwards, Kenny was moved to a two—bed observation room. Pedro was already lying in his bed recovering from surgery, and waiting to see who would be placed in the next bed. They would be sharing the room for a few days. Pedro looked pleased to see Kenny, despite them having never met. Pedro had been worrying about having to share his room with a gypsy. Apparently, Pedro later explained, the local gypsies were very loud. A quiet Englishman was quite a relief.

The pain—killers had long since kicked in. Kenny's thinking was fuzzy. A nurse had put a needle into his arm, with a tube connected to a clear plastic bag. The bag held more pain relief. He'd have to ring back home but that could wait. Tomorrow he'd have a better idea of what was going to happen. His wife would only worry, and after all it was just a broken bone or two.

Kenny's thought's kept returning to the ride and the bike. What could he have done? He felt tired and angry and cheated. It wasn't even a race and he hadn't been going hard.

The medication took hold and Kenny drifted into sleep. Feeling the wheels under him he flew along the coast road. The sky was a beautiful Mediterranean blue and the road ahead was clear.

Later on, it was darker. Kenny could only just reach the nurse call button. Pain forced him into wakefulness. A nurse came quickly, a syringe of morphine. The pain quickly eased, the mind dulled. The pillows felt soft, and moonlight glowed across the mountains, through the window. Kenny's eyes closed heavily as sleep took hold again.

Another day at the Son Llàtzer.

"Buenos Dias, Kennee, Buenos Dias." To the sweetest and softest of voices, Kenny woke up.

An elephant had sat on his shoulder during the night. A dull ache spread across his left side. The face of the nurse, a young Mallorcan woman, looked over him like an angel. Meanwhile, the sun was rising against the backdrop of the Mallorcan mountains.

The nurse held a small plastic cup in her hand and spoke softly again, with the sweetest of voices.

"Kennee, your medicine."

"Analgesics!" She motioned Kenny to take the medicine.

Beside him lay a book: *The Rider* by *Tim*

Krabbé.. Pedro had given it to Kenny the night before saying it would be a good read while he was recovering. Kenny read the blurb on the back cover and smiled.

'Cycling isn't just a metaphor for life, it is life. The journey is unknown, expected and unexpected. The road is waiting.'

Afterword

So you've made it here. Maybe you've taken the short cut, in which case you won't know if Big John found his twenty three seconds or how Tom rides with the Vélo. And if you've come the long way you'll have visited the car park at the Waltzing Weasel and ridden with the Wheelers and Dubrowski, the old pro. You will know Garvey's secret. I remember the hot sweaty afternoon when a Dutch rider held out his hand after he had chased me down in the mountains of Mallorca. These stories started on the road and I would like to thank those riders who have shared the roads with me. I have found the road to be a home and somewhere I feel welcome.

The road is a place where I can find peace, whether cycling around a lake in Sweden, climbing the Tourmalet, or riding a local sportive. Sometimes at night when I'm worried and restless, as my head hits the pillow, I picture the road ahead. Blue skies, a light breeze on my back. I am rolling along a coast road with nothing more than the next café to look forward to. The road is smooth. A rider is just up ahead and I am catching up. Soon I am asleep.

Acknowledgement

My thanks go to Graham Theakston for his help and encouragement. And also to all the riders that have ridden with me as my mind wanders in distant worlds of fantasy and make−believe.

About the author

Kevin Haylett is a cyclist. Like many, he finds cycling a cure for the modern world. It gives him time to think, imagine, and find peace of mind. He lives in Manchester and rides in the hills of the Northwest of England.

"The arts are not a way to make a living. They are a very human way of making life more bearable. Practicing an art, no matter how well or badly, is a way to make your soul grow, for heaven's sake. Sing in the shower. Dance to the radio. Tell stories. Write a poem to a friend, even a lousy poem. Do it as well as you possibly can. You will get an enormous reward. You will have created something."

—Kurt Vonnegut, *A Man Without a Country*

Printed in Great Britain
by Amazon